WHIZ TANNER
and the

Secret
Tunnel

A Tanner-Dent Mystery

Fred Rexroad

Cover Design/Illustration: Alexander T. Lee

Awesome Quest Mysteries

Awesome Quest Mysteries

an imprint of

Rexroad International

Visit us on the web at:
http://Rexroad.International/Awesome

ISBN: 978-1-946650-11-5

To:

Sierra

She knows why

With many thanks to Tara Creel and Michelle Millet, the kind editors at Write On Editing and to Alex Lee for his cover illustration.
A special thanks to Ray for his encouragement and kind words about Whiz and Joey.

References to *Howard Wallace*, PI [978-1454919490, by Casey Lyall, Sterling Children's Publishing] and his list: Rules of Private Investigation, used by permission.

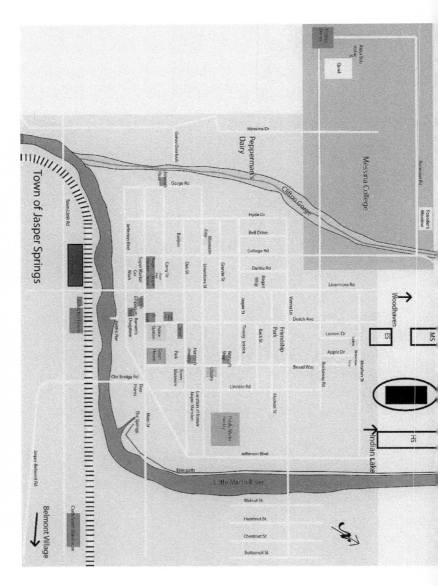

Go to www.WhizTanner.com for a downloadable map
of Jasper Springs.

TABLE OF CONTENTS

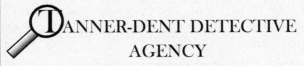

TANNER-DENT DETECTIVE AGENCY

"We solve crimes, mysteries, problems..."

Joseph "Joey" Dent
Director, Field Operations

www.TannerDent.com

TANNER-DENT DETECTIVE AGENCY

"We solve crimes, mysteries, problems..."

Wilson "Whiz" Tanner
Chief Investigator

www.TannerDent.com

CHAPTER 1
What's a DeLorean?

"There's a fight by the bike racks!"

A fifth-grader nearly knocked me down as I left Mrs. Truman's room at the end of the school day. Little kids should treat us sixth-graders with more respect, but I suppose the first good fight of the year got his excitement level skyrocketing. I picked up my pace as I headed to the bike racks myself.

I met Whiz coming out of the counseling center where he spent the last two hours in a pull-out program. Due to his super-duper brainpower, he gets the pleasure of doing harder math and extra stuff while the rest of us do normal classwork. He was about to say something, but I grabbed his arm and pulled him toward the front door.

"Come on."

"Joey, to what do we owe this rough behavior? Detectives should be more discrete."

"There's a fight by the bikes." I continued to pull him along.

"You go on ahead. I need to pick up tomorrow's homework from Mrs. Truman."

If Whiz was anybody else, I would have given him the homework assignment. But Whiz isn't anybody else. In fact, nobody's like Whiz. Mrs. Truman gives him assignments that would scare a middle school kid. They look kinda like ours, but with more parts to figure out and more questions to answer. I couldn't argue with him, so I dropped my grip on his arm.

"I'll see you there." I ran for the door.

When I got to the racks, Parvaneh Shirazi was quickly walking away, while Chuck Boyles and Thorny Rose were deep in a heated argument. Chuck and Thorny are usually pretty close friends, but something got them going. I walked toward them and stopped next to Tommy Whittacker. He was leaning against his bike as we both watched.

"I think a fight's gonna start," said Tommy.

"That's what I heard already. The whole school's heard it." We both looked around at the growing crowd.

"I swear I saw it!" cried Chuck.

The tension eased a bit as Chuck and Thorny saw the group of kids circling them. They seem to be embarrassed by the attention. Slowly, they both pulled their bikes out of the rack.

"No way," said Thorny under his breath, as a last dig.

"It looked just like the one in the movie," yelled Chuck, and the tension started to rise again.

"Yeah, right," said Thorny with his lip curled in a sneer. He turned to me and Tommy. "I mentioned to Parvaneh that *Back to the Future* was coming on TV tomorrow and she could watch it with me ... she's never seen it. Chucky had to one-up me, in front of her, and say he saw the car. She wouldn't know ... she's not from here."

This started to heat up more ... quickly. Thorny's had a not-so-secret crush on Parvaneh since the beginning of the year. She moved to town this summer and was one of the cutest girls in our class—but don't tell Thorny I said that. Anything that got in the way of him making a good impression on her was not gonna go over well.

"What's so hard to believe about that?" Chuck replied. "There are lots of those cars around."

"No way," Thorny shouted over him. "They haven't made them since before we were born, and there aren't any around here. You only said you saw it 'cause I said the movie was going to be on."

"Ask Whiz if it's possible. Hey, Whiz!" Chuck called out, as he spotted Whiz walking our way.

"Yeah, Whiz," Thorny retorted. "Chuck needs some professional help here, but for his head, not from a detective."

"Knock it off, Thorny, and just ask him. You'll see."

"Okay," Thorny replied with a smirk. "Chucky here's been seeing things. He says he saw someone pushing a DeLorean into Farmer Zimmer's barn ... the old one out in his cow pasture. Tell him there's no way. There's not a DeLorean within a thousand miles of Jasper Springs."

"I did see a DeLorean," Chuck yelled back. "Just like the one in the movie *Back to the Future* ... my dad has a poster of it in our garage, so I know what one looks like. Except, it didn't have that flux thingy on the back."

"Ah, the flux capacitor," said Whiz. "The device that turned the car into a time machine. I saw that trilogy of movies last summer ... it was quite a fascinating concept."

Whiz was about to go on when Thorny broke him off. "But are there any of them in Jasper Springs?"

"An interesting question," Whiz said, with a slight squinting of his eyes as if he was thinking deeply about it. "There were not many made, as I recall ... only a couple of model years."

"See, even Whiz says you couldn't have seen one." Thorny gave Chuck a push on the shoulder.

"Now, that is not what I said," responded Whiz. "I said there were not many made. That is a long way from definitively stating there is not one in Jasper Springs."

"Dad says they're still making new ones somewhere in Texas," Chuck said, directly in Thorny's face. "There could easily be one around here."

"No way! They made those in Ireland, and they stopped making them a long time ago. Probably before your dad was even born. My uncle, in California, drove one once and told me all about them. They had doors that opened up like wings, and the body was some special metal that didn't rust, so they didn't need paint." Thorny's face grew red and his voice got louder.

"You can look it up on the Internet if you don't believe me." The volume of Chuck's voice also increased.

Chuck let his bike fall and raised his hand to poke a finger in Thorny's chest. Thorny moved a half a step back, dropped his own bike, and raised his fists.

"Whoa, whoa ..." Tommy rolled his bike between the two but was careful not to get directly between them himself. "Okay, guys ... we can solve this. We have the great Tanner-Dent Detective Agency right here." He smiled and looked over at me and Whiz. "Joey Dent and Whiz Tanner, take a bow."

By this time the group of kids that descended on the bike rack was getting large and they were all hanging around waiting for the fight to start.

"He started it by dissing me in front of Parvaneh ... and he poked me!" Thorny yelled. "You all saw that."

"I don't care how much you like Parvaneh, you called me a liar!" Chuck responded. "I did see one, and they do make new ones in Texas. My dad said so."

"As you stated," said Whiz. "The manufacturing of DeLoreans can be easily verified with a simple Internet search. You have no need of a detective for that."

I turned to the crowd. "Does anybody have a smartphone?"

Nobody pulled one out. I don't think they wanted to stop a fight—we hadn't had a good one yet this year. Or, they knew that here on the north side of town there was no cell coverage, anyway. Either way, very few kids even owned a smart phone, especially those who lived on the northside.

"Yeah, but that's not the point. He said he saw one and that can't be proved since he was the only one there," Thorny responded. "Very convenient for a made-up story, if you ask me."

"I did see one and not because you mentioned the movie, and definitely not because of Parvaneh. Two guys were pushing it into Zimmer's barn, and it can be proved ... just go look in his barn." Chuck began talking to the crowd. "Mr. Zimmer has a DeLorean in his barn, and Thorny is too stupid to believe me."

"What's a DeLorean?" shouted one of the kids.

"It's an old car," yelled another. "Like the time-traveling one in the movie."

"Why's it in his barn? How do you know? Can we see it? What kind of old car? Can it really travel through time?" The calls from the crowd kept coming.

"Tell 'em what you told me," Thorny taunted. "See if they believe you."

So, Chuck began. "Last Saturday, I was riding my bike on Jamestown Road out past Folger's Quarry. It was getting dark, and I was near where the road turns from asphalt to dirt."

"I know the place," called one of the kids. "That's where the abandoned secret Air Force antenna station is."

"That's not secret," responded another kid. "You can see it from the road."

"It used to be secret, back when atomic bombs were secret. The Air Force had them all over the country to catch enemy planes coming to bomb us," replied the first kid.

"Well it's abandoned now," called someone else.

"Or it looks that way because it's so secret. Have you seen all those keep out signs on the tallest chain link fence around?"

"What about the time-traveling car in Farmer Zimmer's barn?" The questions—and answers—continued.

"Yeah, and Mr. Zimmer abandoned that old barn, too," someone else let out. "He hasn't used that barn in years. Nothin' but cows out there."

"They're not cows, they're bulls!" Thorny corrected.

"Well the barn is being used now," Chuck insisted. "There's a car in it ... the famous car from the movies."

"No there's not," Thorny retorted.

"Well, not *the* famous one, but one just like it. I've seen those movies a hundred times, so I know what it looks like. And, I told you, my dad has the poster which I looked at as soon as I got home. The car in Farmer Zimmer's field looked just like it."

"That's simple to check out. Someone has to go to the barn and look," said a kid in the crowd.

"I'm not going up to that barn," Chuck replied. "Thorny may not know much, but he's right about the bulls. Besides, I already saw what's in it."

"Well, I'm not going," responded Thorny with a distinct frown. "Those bulls are mean."

"Hey, I know," called another kid from the crowd. "This is a mystery, so Tanner-Dent can handle it. Mysteries is on their business card, you've seen it. We all have."

Everybody looked at me and Whiz as Tommy said, "Didn't I just say that?"

"Wait a minute," I replied as I thought about the bulls? I didn't want any part of this. "If you think me and Whiz are going—"

"Perhaps the firm of Tanner-Dent could consider this mystery," said Whiz, cutting me off. "However, our services do cost money, and since none of you are currently on retainer, we must decline until such a time as funding has been raised."

With that strange, but typical, response from Whiz, the eagerness seemed to die down a bit, and some of the kids left. Well, that was the end of that—no bull fighting for me. What a relief. Then, I looked over at Whiz. He had that 'staring into space' kinda look he got when he was deep in thought. Uh oh.

"It *would* be interesting to see if Chuck is correct about the DeLorean," Whiz finally said to me, as the crowd thinned out. "I would like to see one up close."

Little did I know, not only did that thoughtful look mean I was going to be investigating Mr. Zimmer's barn, but before our case was over I would come to think that fighting bulls would've been easier!

CHAPTER 2
The Case of the Time-Traveling Car

T he next day, Chuck and Thorny continued to argue about the existence of a car in Farmer Zimmer's barn—and they had help. Support was gaining for both the 'yes there could be a DeLorean' camp—the time-traveling kind or not—and the 'no there can't be a DeLorean' camp. The two sides became known as the McFlys and the Biffs, from the movie.

On Wednesday afternoon, as Thorny mentioned, the first *Back to the Future* movie played on the Jasper Springs Cable Access 2: *Midweek After School Fantastic Movie Break*, which increased the interest in the car. It also caused some of the kids, on Thursday, to change from the no to the yes side. Not because they actually thought the car existed, but because they didn't want to be a Biff.

By Friday morning, the obsession had grown enough that a group of kids pooled their lunch money together to hire Tanner-Dent to find the truth. Whiz, of course, accepted the payment, officially putting Tanner-Dent on the hook to solve the mystery. He never mentioned that we had already planned to make a trip out there on Saturday to check it out for our own—mostly Whiz's—curiosity.

My concern had also quieted by then. I mean, what could be simpler than sneaking up to an old barn and looking inside? We've done that hundreds of times, and now there were a few bucks in it. Easy money, right? One of us had to distract the bulls while the other ran up to the barn—piece of cake. Whiz pocketed the money and we headed to the Crime Lab to stash it in our treasury and plan our weekend.

We rode to Whiz's house and parked our bikes in front of his garage. With all the care of trained detectives, we began our cautious trek to the Crime Lab. The Lab's in an old underground bomb shelter in Whiz's backyard. Our dads, with our help, built a garden shed on top of it. We even made a secret door so we could enter from the back. That's where we headed.

Looking in all directions for spies—you can never be too careful when approaching a location as secret as the Crime Lab—we were satisfied that no one had followed us. So, we sprinted to the back of the shed and crouched near the secret door. Whiz pressed gently on the fake knot in one of the cedar shingles, and a computerized voice sounded from a small hidden speaker.

"Name?" came the computerized whisper.

"Agent M," Whiz responded, just as quietly, into the hidden microphone.

"Password?" came the next command.

"The sun is the nearest star," said Whiz, giving our newest key phrase.

With the correct response given and the voice recognition program finding a match in the database, the computer sent an electric signal to the door lock, and a section of the back wall popped open enough for us to grab. Whiz pulled it wider, and we both entered— Agent M went in, with me, good ol' Agent K, right behind. I pulled the door shut, which triggered the switch to a small black light. This illuminated the white surgical tape on the edge of the stairs, allowing us to walk down safely. At the bottom, we entered through one more door and were inside the Tanner-Dent Detective Agency Crime Lab. Whiz hit the light switch.

As I said before, the Crime Lab is in an old bomb shelter. Some say it was really a storm shelter, but I'm telling the story, and to me it's a bomb shelter—and a big one at that. But, it's our Crime Lab now, complete with all the equipment we need, including a Crime Computer and a growing library. It's amazing, and Whiz and I built it all—well, mostly Whiz, but I helped.

I went directly to the old oak desk where the Crime Computer sat and opened the lower right-hand drawer. Inside was a small metal box containing the Tanner-Dent Treasury. I took it out, placed it on the desk, and lifted the lid. Whiz pulled out all the money the kids at school gave us—mostly coins—and counted it before dumping it in the box. With the Agency financial stuff taken care of, I closed the box and placed it back in the safety of the drawer.

"So, what's our plan, Agent M?" I asked as I stood up.

"Simplicity itself, K. We ride over to Farmer Zimmer's pasture, wait for a chance to sneak up to the barn, when the bulls are elsewhere in the field, and we snap a picture of whatever we see inside." Whiz took his jacket off and threw it over the desk chair.

"What if the door's locked? I would lock the door if I were storing an antique car."

"That should not pose a significant problem. Old barns are notorious for having big cracks and holes everywhere, and the Zimmer barn is probably no exception. I foresee no problem discovering what is inside without the need to actually enter the barn."

"Okay, so when do we start?"

"I suggest we begin our excursion first thing in the morning. Meet me here at eight o'clock." Whiz sat down and turned his attention to the Crime Computer.

"Sounds simple enough. So … I guess I'll see you then." I started for the door. "I'm heading over to the Public Works field. Tommy Whittacker's getting together a pick-up game of football. You coming?"

"You go without me," Whiz replied. "I have some tweaking to do on our security cameras."

Whiz began clicking away at the Crime Computer.

"What security cameras?"

"We have been quite remiss in neglecting a vulnerability in our Headquarters' security."

"How so?"

"Remember how we discussed that we could not ensure our unobserved movement as we were exiting the Crime Lab?"

I didn't remember that conversation, but Whiz has a lot of conversations in his head that he thinks we all can hear. "Not really," I replied.

"Surely, you noticed that there is no way to see outside as we open the door—a spy could ambush us."

"Yeah, I guess." I did notice that, but I don't remember talking about it.

"To solve that problem," continued Whiz. "I mounted two small webcams outside pointing at the secret entrance. We should be able to detect any interlopers before we exit the Lab."

"Interlopers?" That must be one of those Whiz Words he gets from the dictionary—he uses lots of words nobody understands. I think he studies it just to find words I don't know—well, that's not hard to do.

"An interloper is someone who should not be there and may have nefarious intent. With the webcams, we can see them on the Crime Computer before we head out."

I ignored 'nefarious' as I watched him tap a command into the Crime Computer. Two side-by-side pictures appeared on the screen. One showed the back of the shed, secret door and all, and part of the yard between the shed and the garage. The other showed the shed and most of the back yard, including the cedar trees, which lined the Tanner's property. There were no 'interlopers' on the screen.

"They must be charged each morning, and they do not last the entire day ... but it is certainly a start."

"That's pretty cool, Whiz ... uh, Agent M." Sometimes, I still forget to use our code names while in the Crime Lab.

"It was the one remaining flaw in our security system, and now that flaw has been eliminated ... at least partially. I have some adjustments to make in order to maximize the yard coverage. I also want to experiment with a pattern recognition program I found online so that it will sound an alarm if the cameras spot anything that appears human."

He carefully examined the screen and announced, "All clear, Agent K. You can safely exit."

And that's what I did. Once outside I looked around for the cameras but couldn't see them. Then I realized, as I was staring at the roofline of the garage, that Whiz must be watching me and laughing, or whatever he does when others would be laughing. I quit moving my head to look for the cameras and tried to use just eye movements to spot them as I walked over to my bike. With one more unsuccessful look behind me, I took off for the football game.

CHAPTER 3

The Bull Chase

The next morning, at eight o'clock sharp, I was sitting on my bike in Whiz's driveway. He appeared from the back of the shed with a bag strapped over his shoulders—a Surveillance Kit. He climbed on his bike, and we rode up Livermore.

Livermore Road becomes County Road 18 as you leave the city limits and it doesn't get another name until you get to Woodhaven just north of the interstate. Mr. Zimmer owns most of the land west of CR 18, between Messina College and Indian Lake, all the way to the county line—except for Folger's Quarry, the secret abandoned radar site, and a few small lots along the road with houses on them.

Most of the land has crops such as corn, soybeans, or wheat, but a few pastures have animals— mostly normal stuff, like cows and sheep, but Farmer

Cox, who owns a big farm on the east side of CR 18, has llamas and alpacas. It's fun to watch them roam around their field, and every now and then they come close enough to the fence to pet.

The pasture we were interested in, however, had BULLS! Since money and the reputation of the Tanner-Dent Detective Agency were on the line, I rode beside Whiz without ever mentioning that fact.

There was a chill in the air as we rode north, a little bit since it was October and a little bit because— well, I did mention the bulls we were going to meet. About two miles from town, beyond the quarry, is where Jamestown Road crosses. That's where we turned left and headed west.

"There's the barn, Whiz … up on the right."

"I see it, *Agent K.* We have about half a mile to go."

He stressed my code name to highlight that we were on a case and that I didn't use his. I saw it differently.

"But, Whiz, we're not on a case. We got hired to take a picture inside a barn."

"We were hired, as detectives, to solve a mystery, and we should be professional about it."

When he pulls the 'professional' card out of his deck I know better than to argue, so I let it drop.

"I see the bulls, Agent M," I said, as we approached the dirt drive heading into the field.

We turned off the road and stashed our bikes between a tree and some prickly bushes near the ditch that runs along the road. Whiz dug the camera out of the Surveillance Kit before slinging the bag over his handlebars. Since we saw no signs of life, except for the bulls, we walked over to the gate to size up the situation.

"Three bulls and they are on the far side of the barn," said Whiz. "If they stay immobile, we can approach the target without them seeing us. We are also downwind with a slight breeze, which gives us an additional advantage."

"Lucky for us," I said, without really feeling lucky. "We can run up to the barn, snap the shot, and hightail it out before they know we're here. No obstacles."

"Fortuitous, indeed," replied Whiz, with the tinge of excitement in his voice that he seems to get when we're on a case—he was feeling lucky.

But, jeez! Now there was another Whiz Word I would have to look up—it sounds kinda like fortunate, so I'm going with that.

With a nod of his head toward me, we proceeded to climb over the gate. The barn was about a football field length from the road, so I figured I could run the whole distance in about fifteen seconds—a little longer for Whiz—but we did it in stages.

There was an old broken-down wagon about halfway and we ran to it, stopping with it between us and the bulls. So far, so good—except, Whiz began examining the wagon.

"There are some interesting features on this old equipment," Whiz stated, when he saw me looking at him. "The ingenuity they showed in solving—"

"Whiz—Agent M—we're on a case … you said so … and those bulls aren't going to wait for long. As soon as they smell us, our time is up."

This brought Whiz out of his little history daydream.

"Correct you are, Agent K. We have a job to do, however we are downwind from the bulls so the likelihood—"

"Okay, M."

I broke him off again midsentence. That's twice today—a record for me. He gave me a strange look but said nothing more. Turning away, he raised his head to look over the wagon—I did likewise. Whiz turned his attention to the barn, and without much hesitation he headed around the wagon and ran. I followed.

"Agent K, set up an observation post and keep a watchful eye on the bulls. If one of them should make a move toward the barn, sound the alarm so we can evacuate."

Jeez, I sure didn't want to get any closer to the bulls. But, I suppose Whiz was right, we needed to watch them. So, I made my way to the corner of the barn and peeked around.

The three bulls were standing near a tree about as far away from the barn as the barn was from the road. Simple math told me they would have to run twice as fast as to catch me before I could jump the gate. Now the question was, can bulls run twice as fast? I should have checked this with Whiz beforehand.

I kept glancing over to Whiz as he moved from crack to crack in the door and the wall near it. At one point, he moved a loose board that gave him good access for the camera and flash. He had snapped a few pictures when I saw it—a fourth bull!

"Whiz!" I called in a loud whisper. "Bull, nine o'clock."

The fourth bull was walking toward the barn from the other side of the field, and he spotted us. When I called to Whiz, the bull stopped and stared. He also gave some of those snorts you see on TV when the bulls are mad. And we didn't even have a red cape.

"Walk calmly toward the gate, Agent K."

"Calmly? How do we do that with a bull staring us down?"

Whiz didn't answer, but we walked as calmly as we could to the wagon. His stumbling revealed that Whiz was no calmer than I was. We made it to the wagon and ducked down, peeking under to see where the bull was. He was just standing there, snorting. Then, he started moving.

"Wait until the bull gets distracted, then follow my lead, Joey."

I guess code names go out the window when the danger becomes real.

I waited as Whiz threw a dirt clod at the barn. It hit hard, with a thud—did I ever mention that Whiz was the pitcher on our baseball team? Anyway, the bull turned his head, and Whiz made his move.

"Okay, run to the gate. Go!"

We ran! Keeping the wagon between us and the bull as much as possible.

It seemed to work. We couldn't hear the bull moving. And believe me, when that bull moved you could hear—and feel—it. This lasted until we were about halfway between the wagon and the gate—five or six more seconds, I figured.

Then, the bull must have turned to see us running, because he started running. The pounding of the ground was tremendous. The bull got faster, and we got faster—I think.

"Run, M," I yelled, as loudly as I could, but that was completely unnecessary since we were both running as fast as we could already.

I knew I shouldn't—Coach says never to look back while running—but I couldn't resist grabbing a quick peek. Seeing the bull coming at us made my heart pump even faster. That big hulk was getting bigger—he must be gaining!

We both turned on the steam, or so it felt even if our speed didn't really increase. I could feel the ground pounding from the weight of the charging bull, and to make matters worse, the other bulls appeared from around the barn—and they were running. The gate was getting closer, but so were the bulls. In a second and a half, we may be dead!

I reached the gate and jumped over it headfirst without touching. Whiz was right behind but didn't quite make it over the top. I grabbed his arms and pulled as he tried to get a foothold on the bars of the gate. Whiz's foot caught on a brace, and he pushed off with all his strength, a split second before the bull crashed into it. We both tumbled down as the bull slammed into the steel gate. He backed up and just stood there pounding his hoofs and snorting.

"I suggest, Agent K, that we begin our retreat from this place before anybody sees us and wonders why we are riling up these animals."

"I'm more concerned with getting out of here before that bull knocks down the fence."

"That, too," Whiz conceded.

But, he still took the time to aim his camera at the bulls and the barn and snap a few more shots. By then, all four bulls were at the gate, and the biggest one was pushing against it with his head.

We retrieved our bikes and headed back to town—fast. When we had left the pasture behind and neared the turn onto County Road 18, we slowed to a more normal pace.

"Okay, Whiz ... uh, Agent M ... what's the verdict? Did you see a DeLorean in the barn?"

"Our little excursion was a success," he replied. "There is indeed an automobile in the barn, and it does appear to be a DeLorean. I captured several decent photographs which should be sufficient evidence for Thorny and the gang, verifying the existence of the DeLorean."

"Well, success or not, we earned our money on this one," I shot back.

With that, we headed for the Crime Lab, to download the photos, and make a couple of prints for Thorny and Chuck. I think my blood pressure was almost normal when we crossed the town line, near the college. The remainder of the ride back to the Crime Lab was uneventful—didn't we deserve that?

We pulled into Whiz's driveway and dumped our bikes next to the garage. I noticed that Whiz gave a look around at the rooftops of the house and garage.

"What's up, Whiz?"

"Examining the cameras," he replied.

I looked around.

"I still don't see them."

"There are two. The first one, I can reach from my bedroom window, and to reach the second one, I use my dad's stepladder."

He pointed to the top of the house and toward the back of the garage.

I looked harder, and this time, I finally saw the two small webcams mounted under the eaves. They were small—much smaller than I expected—and he'd hidden them pretty well.

"Now, let us see if they did their job."

He darted off to the back of the shed, pressing the fake knot. I was right beside him as we entered and climbed down the steps. Whiz rushed to the Crime Computer, sat down, and hit a few keys. I moved in behind him and looked over his shoulder.

"Look at us," he said, pointing to the screen. "I left it on record while we were gone, and it shows us leaving. Further on we should be seen coming back."

Sure enough, there we were. I was on my bike at the edge of the driveway, and Whiz was running from behind the shed toward me. We both left the camera range, and the feed from both just showed the empty yard. Whiz hit a key, and the two shots went into fast forward. A few minutes later we saw Tammy, Whiz's younger sister, running out of the house followed closely by Mrs. Tanner. They entered the garage, and we saw the car back out.

After that, nothing much happened, other than a cat and a couple of squirrels scurrying through the yard, until we returned, a few moments ago. Whiz slowed it to normal speed, and there we were, looking at the cameras and pointing.

"That's cool, Whiz ... uh, Agent M. Just like that time at the town museum. We should find a way to use these on a case."

"Hidden cameras would make a very useful tool after we devise a process for employing them. As I said, I want to adjust the view of each camera and recharging is a problem, but essentially, they are operational. Now, back to the current case."

He connected the camera to the Crime Computer and turned it on. The pictures downloaded automatically.

"Now, we shall see if we captured sufficient evidence." As he spoke, he brought the first picture up full screen on the monitor.

CHAPTER 4
Another Successful Case

The picture was too dark to make anything out—perhaps a dark blob the size of a car. This was not going to be exciting enough to stay standing. I pulled over a folding chair and sat behind Whiz. It was only after sitting, that I realized the rush from the bulls chasing me had worn me out.

I skootched in closer to the desk beside Whiz, as he clicked through the pictures v e r y s l o w l y. The cracks in the barn were too small to let in light from the flash, so the only light was from other cracks. While there were many of them, they were not so plentiful that they lit up the inside of the barn much.

In some, you could see the dark shape of a car, but not enough to say it was a DeLorean, or any particular car, for that matter. Finally, Whiz got to the shots he snapped after moving one of the boards. Now the flash worked, and we could see much more.

"Agent K! Look at this photograph!"

Whiz practically knocked me out of my chair as he turned.

"Okay, that looks like a DeLorean to me," I responded.

We'd seen enough pictures, on many websites, that we were now experts on what a DeLorean looked like.

"You are missing the vital clue in this scene. Look closely, and use your detective brain."

I looked again. It was a picture of the inside of Farmer Zimmer's barn. In the center was a silver colored car that appeared to be a DeLorean—I was sure of that. The rest of the place was pretty much empty— kinda like you would expect to see in an abandoned barn, except for a few small piles of dirt, some car parts off to the side, and what looked to be a ladder sticking into a hole in the ground at the left edge of the picture, near the piles of dirt.

"What clue, Whiz?" I purposely didn't use his code name to stress that I didn't see any mystery. "We proved there's a DeLorean in Famer Zimmer's barn, but that was nothing to get super excited about. We got paid to look, and we looked. The money's the same no matter what we found."

"Pay particular attention to the dirt piles in this picture, Agent K ... and the hole. When you correlate those facts, it becomes obvious."

"Okay, so it's obvious." Then, I thought some more, and it wasn't obvious. "What is it?"

Whiz looked at me like I was a kindergartner and shook his head—except he never looked at Tammy that way, and she was a kindergartner.

"Detectives observe their surroundings, Agent K. There are several piles of dirt near the hole. That hole is most probably where the dirt making up those piles originated."

"But that's not a mystery. We were sent to find a car, not a dirt pile ... or a hole in the ground," I replied.

"The mystery, K, is why would Farmer Zimmer dig a hole in his barn?" Whiz asked.

"He wanted some place to dump used oil from the car or dump some garbage. Mr. Reynolds tried to do that so he didn't have to pay the town to take away his garbage anymore," I offered.

Whiz did not look amused—and I'm sure, Mr. Reynolds wasn't either. He had to pay a huge fine and dig out all the garbage.

"But the hole has a ladder sticking out of it. It must be quite deep to require a ladder. I deduce that Farmer Zimmer added a secret room under his barn ... a room big enough to need a ladder to climb down into."

"Yeah, I guess. Maybe he needed more storage."

"More storage, Agent K? Look at all these photographs. That is a big barn, and while we cannot see the western side, the rest is nearly empty ... except for the automobile. Why would he need more storage than what is already there?"

"Uh, because ..."

I couldn't think of a because, but I still didn't think there was anything unusual about it.

"He has built a clandestine room under his barn," continued Whiz. "Why would he need that in a barn that has been otherwise deserted for years?"

"What kinda room?"

"Clandestine … concealed, hidden, possibly for some nefarious intent."

"Okay, okay, Agent M," I humored him. "So, Farmer Zimmer made an underground room in his old barn. Why do we care? He's allowed to have a secret underground room. We have one." I waved my hand around to indicate the Crime Lab we were sitting in. "And, it doesn't look so *clandestine* with a ladder sticking out of it. Besides, we don't know that it's a whole room. It could be just a deep hole."

This seemed to take the wind out of him. But, at the same time, I was now getting a bit curious. If Farmer Zimmer has a secret underground room, I do kinda want to know what's in it.

"I suppose you are correct, Joey." He dropped the code name, so I knew I got to him. "It has been a couple of weeks since we had a good mystery to occupy our brains. Maybe, I just wanted one."

"Well, we just solved one, so let's print off a few copies of these pictures and close this case … the Case of the Silver Car."

But even as I said it, I was thinking about that hole. I'm sure Whiz was too.

Whiz hit the print button to make several copies of the best shot—the DeLorean was unmistakable. This would prove to Thorny, and the other kids, that Chuck was telling the truth, and we could keep our payment in the company treasury with good conscience. How Thorny makes up for looking foolish in front of Parvaneh, I don't know—we can't solve everything.

I picked up three of the prints, folded and stuffed them into my back pocket, and turned toward the door of the Lab when I noticed Whiz was still staring at the pictures on the Crime Computer screen. He was clicking between inside and outside shots. I snapped my fingers a few times before he broke his concentration and looked up at me.

"Are we going, or what?" I asked.

I waited a moment while he came back to the real world. Whiz has the weird ability to be in his own little world and ignore other people sometimes—like they aren't there. And, he's a bit startled when he realizes they actually are. Usually it's not so bad, but today it was.

"Something else is bothering me about these photographs."

"What?"

"Wire … but we will get to that later, Agent K. We have evidence to deliver."

With that, he seemed to snap out of his little episode and became his ol' cryptic self. But, I too was thinking more about the hole. And wire? What does that have to do with the barn? These questions began rattling around my brain as Whiz switched the Crime Computer screen to show the outside webcams.

"The exit is clear." He got up and walked to the door.

"Right, M." I fell in behind.

Given that it was not quite lunchtime on a Saturday, the obvious location was where we headed first. We found Thorny and Chuck at the field outside the Public Works department. A typical Saturday pick-up game of football had just ended, and the two of them were tossing the ball back and forth as they walked toward us. We dropped our bikes at the edge of the field and walked out to meet them.

"Hey, are you guys going out to Zimmer's farm now?" asked Chuck. "I want to come and watch you fight the bulls."

"Too late. We're done," I replied.

"I'll bet you didn't find anything, did you?" said Thorny. "Nobody would keep a valuable car in a rundown barn. There's nothing in it, and you couldn't see in anyway."

"You are wrong on both counts, Thorny." Whiz said, as I handed a picture to each guy. "Mr. Zimmer's barn contains an automobile, and it is indeed a DeLorean."

Thorny's face dropped noticeably as he looked at the picture. "A lot of kids at school are going to be disappointed."

"You most of all," Chuck said with a big smile. He then tossed the football to Thorny. "It's lunchtime and I'm hungry."

Thorny agreed, and the two headed off, while Whiz and I walked back to our bikes.

"So, you want to jump into a training exercise after lunch?" I asked.

"Agent K, we have a case to solve. What better training is there than a real live case?" he replied.

"What case? We just closed our only case."

"Meet me at the Crime Lab after lunch," he said, as he grabbed his bike and took off.

I stared after him, as I got on my bike. What case were we on now? What information did Whiz get that he thinks we have a new case to solve? This must have something to do with that hole. Oh, well, no time to waste on that thought, I was hungry too. I headed home for lunch, where I had to make a sandwich for myself. Everybody else had stuff to do and was gone, so Mom left me a note.

The note was instructions for making myself lunch—as if I didn't know how to spread peanut butter on bread and then cover it with jelly. She even added that I needed to cut it diagonally. Jeez. Moms. What are you gonna do? I made the sandwich and ate it. Not bad.

When I had finished eating, I cleaned up, put the milk, peanut butter, jelly, and bread away. And, that part wasn't even in the instructions! I cleaned myself up—peanut butter is sticky, you know—and headed out. It was an uneventful ride over to Whiz's house, and in short order, I was in the Crime Lab, where I found Whiz sitting at the oak desk clicking away at the Crime Computer.

"Well, Agent M, what's up? What's our new case?"

"Wire, Agent K," he responded.

"The wire in Farmer Zimmer's barn?" I asked. "How's that a case?"

"Look at this."

He turned the monitor so I could have a better look, then pressed a few keys and sat back. There was a picture of the outside of the barn. It must have been one of the pictures he took after we escaped the bulls. He spun the wheel on the mouse to enlarge the photo.

"Do you see the wire running from the ground up the side of the barn and into a hole near the last horse stall?"

I looked. Sure enough, there was a thick wire that looked like the electric wire running to my house from a utility pole in the back yard.

"Okay." I replied. "So, what?"

He moved the photo to focus in on the ground next to the barn.

"You can still see the line of overturned soil from the point where the wire enters the ground to the wooded area. It must be newly buried, and it is certain that the new wire and the new deep hole inside the barn are connected. So, why would Farmer Zimmer run electricity into an abandoned barn and then down into the hole?"

"That doesn't seem so interesting to me," I responded. "Anyway, you have no reason to believe the wire and the hole are connected. Maybe he wants lights in the barn ... to work on the car at night, or power tools, or something."

Whiz brought up another picture.

"What do you see, Agent K?"

It was one of the shots taken of the inside of the barn.

"That's a picture of the DeLorean inside the barn," I responded.

"And?"

"It shows the hole, with a ladder in it and some piles of dirt around it. We already knew all that."

"But, what do you see running down the support beam, through that box, across the ground, and into the hole?"

"Oh," I said, after looking more carefully. "An electric wire."

"Precisely. That wire points to a mystery, Agent K. There must be a reason for electricity in the hole."

"Lights," I answered. "If he has a room, he will need to light it."

"That wire carries 240 volts of electric current. Lights only require 120," Whiz stated. "There must be something big in that hole to use 240 volts. We must find out what. We will use this as a grand training exercise."

I was once again beginning to get interested in what's in the hole. Of course, I also love the excitement of a new case, but I couldn't help thinking of the bulls.

"Remember the bulls, Agent M? Whadda we do about them?"

"An excellent point. I have just the remedy for that."

"What?" I had to know what dangerous thing he had planned for us.

"Camouflage."

"Camouflage?" I asked, not convinced that would lessen the danger.

"Conceal. Blending into the surroundings. Hiding."

"I know what camouflage is. I'm just wondering how that'll help us run from a stampeding bull. You don't have an invisibility cloak—do you? That's what we really need."

I could think of many things we could do better with an invisibility cloak. Why are the good things only available in fiction books? If we had an invisibility cloak
. . .

"The idea," said Whiz, bringing me out of my daydream, "is to not be detected by the bulls. I have some ideas that I have been kicking about that will help us sneak around unobserved. I think it is high time we started testing those ideas."

"You seriously want to sneak around, undetected by a herd of bulls?"

"Four bulls do not make much of a herd, K. But, bulls are no more intelligent when it comes to identifying a foe than people are. Smell, sound, and sight, are the only senses we need to worry about, and two of them we have a great deal of control over. The third one ... I have some ideas about."

"And what're those?"

"Later, Agent K. I have some research and experimentation I want to get to. In the meantime, you can be thinking about what possible things Farmer Zimmer could be doing inside that hole. That will give us a heads up on what we may find—the fewer surprises the better."

With that he turned back to the Crime Computer and began typing away. I could see that he had slipped well into Whiz World, so I took this as my cue to leave him to it. There was probably a football or soccer game going on somewhere, anyway. I quietly slipped out the door of the Crime Lab after Whiz assured me no 'interlopers' were hanging around his backyard.

CHAPTER 5
Thinking—All Part of Detective Work

As I walked toward my bike, trying to think about what I would do in a hole, in a barn, I decided the best place to think about that would be at Barnett's Drug Store while sipping a root beer float.

When I arrived at Keith's Pier, across from the drugstore, Tommy Whittacker and Ray Michielini, were sitting on the edge of the dock dangling their feet just above the water. It was much too cold to get wet, but dangling your feet still seemed like a nice thing to do.

I parked my bike and sat down next to them. Tommy was in my class at school, but Ray, whose dad was a lieutenant on the Jasper Springs Police Force, was a few years older and already in high school. He lived next door to Tommy, and nobody dared to mention it now, but Ray used to babysit him. Nowadays, Ray kinda watches out for him—none of the big guys pick on Tommy.

"What's up, guys?" I asked.

"Chuck called me and said you and Whiz took a picture of the DeLorean in Farmer Zimmer's barn," Tommy said.

"Yup," I responded. "We had to fight off four mean bulls, but it was nothing that Tanner-Dent couldn't handle. As you see, we got out alive."

"You guys went into Farmer Zimmer's bull pasture?" asked Ray.

"You bet. Nothing will keep the Tanner-Dent Detective Agency from performing its duty. Especially if money's involved."

"They were settling a bet between Thorny and Chuck," Tommy informed Ray. "Chuck said he saw a DeLorean in Zimmer's barn, and Thorny, who thinks he's a DeLorean expert since his uncle drove one once, didn't think there could be one in Jasper Springs."

"What's a DeLorean?" asked Ray.

"You know … a car … like the one in the movie *Back to the Future*," Tommy replied.

"Oh, the time-traveling movie. The one on TV last week."

"That's it," I said. "We saw one too. Of course, it was just a normal car. We took a picture to prove it." I pulled the last picture out of my pocket and handed it to Tommy.

"How'd you get around the bulls?" asked Tommy.

"Oh, we have our ways … you just have to outsmart them. It was easy until we got chased, but we're working on other ways to get around them so it doesn't happen again."

"Again? Are you going back?" asked Tommy.

"You got the picture. Chuck said Thorny was satisfied that the car is there."

"While you're solving mysteries," Ray broke in, as he looked at the photo. "Do you know why there's a ladder in a hole next to the car? Does the barn have a basement?" He chuckled.

"No, we never got close enough to see in the hole. We didn't know it was there until we saw the photo."

"To me, that's more of a mystery than an old car," said Ray.

"Yeah, Whiz thought that, too."

"So, you're going back?" asked Tommy.

"Maybe. You know how Whiz is. I'm sure it's nothing, but he might want to drag me back there just to investigate. Anyway, we got the bull thing covered."

"Yeah, I'd go back," announced Ray.

Uh oh. I definitely said too much. I need to downplay this, quickly.

"Well, you know, only as a training exercise. Gotta keep our investigative skills in tiptop shape."

My brain told me to leave before I said any more and got their curiosity up too much.

"I'm gonna head in for a root beer float. See you guys later."

I grabbed the photo and left quickly before they could offer to join me and pry out any more information about the hole. I left my bike in the Keith's Pier bike rack and ran across the street. After ordering the root beer, I made my way to our usual booth, sitting with my back to the wall, so I could see the entire store, and began sipping my drink—and thinking.

I tried to come up with good reasons to dig a hole inside a barn, but I couldn't come up with anything useful. If there were pipes or something running under his field, well maybe, he was digging down to repair them. But, I saw two problems with this.

First, pipes wouldn't be that deep. I've watched my dad and his crews digging up pipes many times—the guys are only a little bit below the street level as they work on them. And second, why would there be pipes running through his bull pasture in the first place. The water trough for the bulls was next to a small windmill, at the far end of the pasture, that pumped the water from the ground. There were no houses, or even other barns anywhere nearby—only the Air Force place next door, but I'm sure their water pipes, if they had any, would be by the road, not running under Farmer Zimmer's pasture.

After about fifteen minutes, I finally gave up. I had finished my root beer float, so it was time to go. As I was getting up, Mr. Lovett came toward the booths with a tray of food. He worked for my dad at the town Public Works.

"How ya doing, Joey?" he asked in his usual friendly way. "Did your dad get all his garden stuff packed away? He mentioned on Friday that winterizing around your house was his big weekend project."

"Uh, not yet, Mr. Lovett," I answered. "Tomorrow though. I'm helping."

It was then I noticed the patches sewn onto the old jacket he wore. He always wore it, but today I noticed that most of the patches had Air Force logos on them—planes, propellers, missiles, lightning bolts, things like that.

"Were you in the Air Force, Mr. Lovett?" I asked, as a thought began forming in my brain.

"Sure was. Retired years ago, that's when I moved back to Jasper Springs."

This connection got me thinking. "Do you know anything about the abandoned Air Force Station out past Farmer Zimmer's bull pasture."

"Of course, it's an old SAGE Station. They decommissioned it back in the early 1960s. Well before my time in the Air Force. But, when I was a kid, there was still some activity out there."

"What's a sage?"

"It was a radar station. SAGE stands for Semi-Autonomous Ground Environment. The SAGE Radar. It was part of the system of radar and radio antenna stations scattered throughout the country to watch the skies. All that technology became obsolete rather quickly. With satellites and much more advanced electronics, we can watch the world much better."

"If they abandoned the station, why does it still have a really tall fence around it? And, the keep out signs?"

"They decommissioned and removed the radar but the station is still active. The Air Force turned most of the old stations over to local communities for parks and other types of development. The ones that remain still have a use for the Air Force."

"So, the Air Force still uses that station out by Farmer Zimmer's pasture?"

"It's classified work, so I don't know what goes on, but they send a small crew out there a couple of times a month for something. I've seen them going in, but I have no idea what they do there."

Boy, Whiz was going to love to hear this. The old secret Air Force Station is still secret. Maybe they keep aliens there! Maybe they store all the secret plans for new jets and rockets in an underground bunker— what a sneaky place to hide secrets! I needed to get this information to Whiz.

"Well, thanks for the stories, Mr. Lovett." I turned to head out.

"My pleasure, Joey. Say hi to your dad for me."

I left as quickly as I could without looking too suspicious. Once outside, I ran to my bike and took off. Tommy and Ray, were not on the pier anymore, so I didn't have to worry about them.

I skidded to a halt in Whiz's driveway and rushed to the back yard. After the correct sequence, I entered the Crime Lab, but it was empty. I quickly left, ran to the house, and pressed the back doorbell a few times. No answer. Maybe he was at the library—he used to practically live at the library. So, I took off—full speed—on my bike.

The library was a bust and I ran out of places to look—he must be out with his parents somewhere. Since the Public Works field was close by and there was sure to be another game of football underway, I headed over there. This added a good two hours of distraction to my day. After the game, I rushed back to the Crime Lab, but still no Whiz. Another ring of his doorbell also got nowhere.

The Air Force Station not being abandoned couldn't have anything to do with Farmer Zimmer's barn anyway, so I'll just mention it tomorrow. Whiz might have two or three other mysteries to solve by then instead of a hole in a barn.

Reluctantly, I headed home to supper—and a quiet evening watching TV with my sister, Patty, who, of course, had a book opened the whole time. College has turned her a little bit into Whiz.

CHAPTER 6
The New Case Forms

Sunday morning was fairly quiet, and after church, Mom served us her wonderful roast beef with potatoes, carrots, and some little round vegetables that I don't know the name of—she used the self-timer on the oven to cook it while we were gone. It sure beat the peanut butter and jelly sandwich I had yesterday. As usual, Mom really went all out for Sunday lunch. Then, the chores began.

With fall well underway, Dad wanted to prepare everything for winter, so I found myself helping with outdoor cleanup. Dad had already gone down in the basement to shut the water valves to the outside spigots, while I opened them up to drain the remaining water. We folded up the lawn chairs and put them in the rafters of the garage. The patio table took a bit longer, since we had to dismantle it to stash it in its winter home at the back of the garage. I drained the last drops of water from the garden hose and was rolling it up, when Dad called over to me.

"Joey, look at that." Dad pointed to the sky. "Some kid must have let go of his balloon."

I looked up. A red balloon floated over Mr. Carlisle's house, my backdoor neighbor. It was about thirty feet up and still rising when it got overhead. I watched as it sailed south over my house. As I turned my attention back to rolling up the last garden hose, another balloon, a blue one, caught my eye. I watched this one with much more interest.

Excitement grew in my body as I turned toward Mr. Carlisle's house and saw another red balloon floating over. I grabbed the rolled-up hose and hurried toward the garage. It was the last of the prewinter chores.

"Hey, Dad," I yelled, as I walked quickly to my bike. "If you're finished with me, I'll be going to Whiz's."

"I think that'll do it, son. Have a good time, but remember, supper is going to be late tonight, but don't *you* be late for it. Also, it's a school night."

Mom was having one of her committee meetings tonight, so Dad was in charge of cooking. He hated anytime I was late for supper, but even more so when he was cooking. I assured him I would be home, on time, before jumping on my bike and racing down the alleyway. As I turned onto College Road, I gave a quick look for the kid who lost the balloons, but I was pretty sure I wouldn't see him.

The balloons were a message from HQ. I knew it the moment I saw it. Three balloons—red, blue, red—means report to the Crime Lab, ASAP. Agent M must have discovered a breakthrough in our case—if we're on a case. Maybe he saw something new in one of the photographs.

I screeched to a halt in Whiz's driveway and almost toppled over as my bike stopped just a tiny bit before I did. Nobody saw me, and I recovered nicely. I pushed the kickstand down with my right foot and ran to the back of the shed.

"Name?" came the response, after I pressed the fake knot.

"Agent K."

"Password."

Uh oh. Whiz changed the pass phrase last night, and I forgot what he told me it would be. Something about—atoms. That's it, atoms. We started studying them in school last week. I had to say something before the Crime Computer program timed out.

So, I said, "Protons are … tiny."

There was a short pause, but not the clicking sound that I was hoping for. Then, I heard through the hidden speaker, "Intruder sequence has begun."

This was new to me, and I could hear a faint siren from inside the Crime Lab. In a few seconds, it stopped, and a rather irritated voice—Whiz's voice—came over the speaker.

"Agent K, you must be more attentive to security protocol." Followed by an irritated sounding, "Enter!"

The latch clicked, and the secret door popped open a few inches. I grabbed it, opened it farther, and went in. When I came through the door at the bottom of the steps, I found Whiz, uh, Agent M, standing by the work table with his arms folded, staring at me.

"Neutrons have no charge!"

Ah, yes. That was it. Neutrons, protons, electrons—I knew it was one of those three.

"Sorry. I'll get it next time."

Without any more discussion, Whiz threw a pair of brownish pajamas, full of dark blotches, at me.

"What are these?"

"Surveillance Suits. I repurposed two old pajamas for our next excursion to the barn."

"These are the ugliest pajamas I've ever seen. Where did you get them?"

"They are two of my old ones. You have seen them plenty of times. I did, however, dye them to blend into the wooded background we need to traverse."

"What are we doing in the background?" I eyed the brown pajamas as I held them up—only half listening to Whiz.

"Traversing the woods. We need to cross through the wooded area on the western side of Farmer Zimmer's pasture. That will give us the best chance of scoping out the situation without being seen."

"Oh." I looked more closely at the pajamas. "I guess they do look a little familiar ... without the dye job."

"I mixed several used boxes of dye Mom had left over from a tie-dye project at Tammy's kindergarten. When you mix many different colors, you end up with a muddy brown ... just perfect for our stealthy purposes. We will sneak into the woods, put these on, and then camouflage our exposed skin."

There's that word again. "Camouflage?" I asked. "This is how we're going to sneak past the bulls?"

"Precisely, Agent K. We will cover our faces and hands with something that will blend into our surroundings, adding the same protection as the Surveillance Suits."

"Are you talking about face paint, M?"

"Paint, yes. There is a sample-size jar of brown wall paint in the garage ... a flat latex that should work nicely and not reflect light."

He stuffed his brown pajamas—uh, Surveillance Suit—in his Surveillance Kit and threw a second backpack to me.

"Here is a Surveillance Kit I outfitted for you. It has a flashlight, a knife, some rope, and a few other useful items. Put your Surveillance Suit in there, and tonight we will begin our excursion."

"Tonight? Is that why you called me here with a secret message?"

"Yes, Agent K. New clues have presented themselves." He glanced at the camera feeds and started toward the door.

"What new clues?"

He stopped and turned toward me. "I examined the pictures we took inside the barn with an extra level of diligence, and I saw more than we first were able to discern."

"You found something more than the hole? What?"

"No, Agent K. It was still just a hole. However, the hole has been reinforced with wooden sides. If you examine carefully, you can see the wooden reinforcement."

"But, how does that change anything, M?"

"This proves the hole is very deep, and significant work went into making sure it does not collapse. Also, there is a pulley attached to a beam directly above the hole. Perhaps this aided in removing loads of dirt from the bottom. However, it is quite a sizable pulley, made for a lot of weight. They must have been extracting a lot of dirt in order to make such a massive pulley system necessary. Of course, we already knew about the electric wire running into it. Tanner-Dent must investigate this."

"Okay," was all I could think to say.

I hoped this didn't backfire—we didn't need to get on the wrong side of a bunch of bulls, herd or not, just to look inside a hole.

We left the Crime Lab and stopped by the garage on our way to the bikes. In there, Whiz found the small jar of brown paint and placed it gently in his Kit. We were ready.

The ride out to Zimmer's farm, was uneventful. As we did yesterday, we rode a couple of miles and turned left on Jamestown Road. This time we passed the gate to Farmer Zimmer's pasture and continued to the woods on the other side. An additional problem faced us immediately. The bulls, all four, were together near the eastern edge of the pasture—which was great. But, there was an old pickup truck parked in front of the barn door.

"Bad luck, M. We can't explore the hole now."

"On the contrary, Agent K, now is the best time. If we can get to the barn undetected, we may be able to overhear what is happening inside."

Whiz pushed his bike into the brush beside the road, and I followed—not very enthusiastically, I might add. Anyway, after hiding our bikes in the ditch at the edge of the fence line, we climbed into the pasture. Here, there was about thirty feet of woods between the tall chain link fence at the edge of the abandoned Air Force Station and the open pasture of Farmer Zimmer's field—nothing else between there and the barn, except maybe bulls.

"As I presumed," said Whiz. "Based on prevailing winds, the air flow is in our favor. The bulls will not be able to smell us … one of three vital senses taken care of. Let us proceed."

"But what about the truck?" I was getting more worried the farther we got from the road.

"We will take necessary precautions as the situation dictates, Agent K." He threw in Agent K to play on my sense of professionalism. "From here on, we must be very quiet. That will be the second of the senses we must guard against."

We walked the fence line to a small clearing about level with the barn. We pulled the Surveillance Suits out of the Kits and put them on over our clothes. The suits were a little tight and definitely would not go over our jackets, but they gave us a little bit of warmth. Whiz twisted the lid off the jar of paint and dipped a small square of cloth into the brown liquid.

"Let me apply this to hide your face," he said, as he shoved the cloth toward me. "It will be dark soon, and our trek to the barn will be fully concealed. The third of the senses that must be addressed."

I didn't have much say in this, and before long, the drying paint completely covered my face. I took the square of cloth and did the same to Whiz. Then, we each painted the backs of our own hands. It had a weird smell, and as it dried it felt stiff and strange. I reminded myself that at least we weren't going to get close enough to the bulls to worry about the last two senses—touch and taste!

We stuffed a few items from the Surveillance Kits—such as two flashlights and a camera—into pockets that Whiz had sewn onto the pajamas. After stuffing our jackets into the Kits, we sat in the clearing and waited for darkness. The paint was getting drier and stiffer. A short time later, we crawled to the edge of the woods and waited some more. The truck was still there. I thought that was unlucky, but Whiz was even more excited.

As we waited, I thought I heard a strange noise—well, more felt it than heard it.

"Agent M," I said. "Do you feel that pounding?" I knelt and placed my hands on the ground.

"I do feel something. It reminds me of the vibration from that jackhammer the guys used to break up the sidewalk in front of the *Jasper Springs News* office last summer. You could feel it a block away."

"Yeah, that's what I thought. It sounds far away. Where do you think it's coming from?"

Whiz placed his ear against the ground and listened.

"I cannot discern its location. But, we can investigate that later. For now, we must continue on our original quest."

So, we continued … to wait.

CHAPTER 7
The Case Gets Bigger

When it was dark enough, Whiz started crawling. Of course, I was right next to him. Crawling from the west, in the darkening twilight, we kept the barn between us and the bulls all the way up to the barn wall. We moved very slowly so that quick movements wouldn't catch the eye of anybody, or any bull, casually looking in our direction.

Our Surveillance Suits blended into the brownish grass and bare dirt spots of the pasture, so we felt safe edging up to the barn. It was getting quite dark, which in one sense added to our feeling of safety, but in another, made it seem a little more dangerous.

But at last, we were at the barn and all set. We agreed to use hand signals to communicate once we got to the barn, just in case there *was* someone inside which required us to be very quiet.

What we didn't realize was, with not much moonlight and no streetlights, it would be too dark to see hand signals. I realized this as we arrived at the barn, and I wanted to tell Whiz to go slowly—but that wasn't Whiz. Oh, well, something new to add to our manual— the Tanner-Dent Compilation of Useful Detective Tactics, Tricks, and Procedures. We call it the TTP, for short, and add to it after every case.

I followed Whiz as he crawled along the barn wall looking for a way to see in. We rounded the corner and made it almost to the big door on the back side when we found a missing board leaving a six-inch gap almost three feet in length.

Carefully, I climbed around Whiz, and we both stuck our heads as far as we could into the gap. There was a dim light somewhere inside, but it was still too dark to see anything—something was in the way.

There was also talking inside. Mostly mumbles, but every now and then, I could make out some real words.

"There are at least two guys in there, M," I said softly, but of course, he already knew that.

I tapped his shoulder and pointed to indicate we should head back to the safety of the woods, but he had a different plan. He was pulling on a loose board next to the gap.

"What are you doing?" I asked, in a whisper.

"I am trying to make a hole big enough to allow us to enter the barn," he replied, to my growing horror.

At this point, the board gave way with a low, but noticeable thud. He stopped, as we both listened. The faint muffled talk continued so it appeared they didn't hear us. I breathed a sigh of relief as Whiz carefully set the board down and examined the new hole.

"Good fortune has smiled on us, Agent K. They must be down in the hole and unable to hear anything up here, and now this opening is sufficient to permit our entry."

And ... he started to enter!

Of course, I pushed in right behind him. It took a bit of pushing, too, to move the stack of three hay bales that was in our way. We pushed them in about two feet. The light got brighter as the bales moved away from the wall. When we had enough room to climb in and stand, we quit pushing. By standing, we were just tall enough to see over the bales.

Several small lights were hanging around the barn with one directly over the hole. We were in a shadow near the wall, but with our eyes used to the night, it was like daytime in the barn. Let me tell you, we were quite surprised at what we saw. Now, this was a pretty big barn and even had stalls for horses and other animals—but, in addition to the DeLorean sitting near the front door, it was nearly full with big mounds of dirt.

Very quietly, we looked around to make sure nobody else was there—nobody was. We still heard muffled talking coming from the hole along with strange sounds as if they were dragging something.

"That hole must be deeper than we thought," I whispered.

"Definitely," was all Whiz said in reply. Then, he started climbing over the hay bales. "We need a better look."

Whiz dropped to the other side, and I climbed over, after he settled down without raising suspicion from the hole.

"What are we going to do?" I asked.

"I want a picture of the inside of that hole."

"You're not going down there." My whisper got louder.

"We shall see."

He walked carefully over to the hole with his camera at the ready. Pointing it down the hole, he took a couple of pictures—no flash.

"So, what's down there?"

"The hole gets bigger at the bottom."

He was about to say more when we heard the dragging sounds again, and they were getting louder.

"I think they're coming back, Whiz, uh, M," I said, a bit flustered. "We should scram!"

"I agree … go."

We climbed over the hay bales and hunkered down in the dark. As we stooped in our hiding place it dawned on me that they might notice how far the bales were from the wall. But, the first guy had just come out of the hole so I didn't dare tell this to Whiz. We also didn't dare climb out through the missing boards—they would have heard that noise.

"Send the bucket down," one guy said.

"Watch your head," the other replied.

Whiz edged around the bales as far as he dared to see what was happening—I did the same. A guy was pulling on a rope, which went around a pulley and was tied to a big bucket. It came out of the hole, full of rocks, which he dumped into a wheelbarrow before sending the bucket back down.

This went on for several minutes. When the wheelbarrow was full, he took it toward the back of the barn and dumped it—even though there wasn't much space left to dump with all the dirt piled up.

After a few of these trips the guy at the bottom yelled, "last one," and the guy at the top pulled it up. He went to dump the wheelbarrow as the other guy climbed out.

"We're through, Donald! Woo-hoo!" His hands raised in the air like he was doing a victory dance.

"This is only step one, Cal," the wheelbarrow guy replied. "And you should keep your voice down."

"There's nobody around for miles to hear us." And, to prove his point he yelled, "Woo-hoo," again. This time at the top of his lungs.

"This is not the time to celebrate, Cal. The most dangerous part is still ahead of us."

"Yeah, I know. We're tangling with something kinda big, and that worries me," said Cal. "So, I get to do my touchdown dance to mark closer to the end."

"Get over it," replied Donald. "It's too late for a queasy stomach … the hard work is done. The important part is all that's left. Then … we're gone."

"What about my DeLorean? I've been working on it for over two years, and I'm nearly finished with the restoration. The engine is almost running, and after I buff out the scratches on the front fender, it'll be perfect. What do I do with it when the time comes to disappear?"

"Forget about the car."

"But I love that car. It's my hobby. I built that car from parts I found at junk yards all over the country, and I'd be done by now if you didn't get me involved in this."

"In a month, you'll be too rich for hobbies … and for worries."

"But that car's the whole reason ol' man Zimmer's letting us use this barn. We're paying him good money to let me rebuild here and I'm not leaving it behind. Heck, we could've probably done all this without paying him a dime or using my car as a decoy. He hasn't set foot in here in years. He hasn't even come to look at the car. He would've never known. One of his hired hands comes to feed the bulls, but even he doesn't come near the barn."

"As I've said before, the cost of that car, and the pittance we're paying Zimmer, is chicken feed compared to what we'll get when this is over."

"And you're sure what's over there is going to make us rich?"

"Beyond your wildest dreams. After months of digging, we're almost there. Busting through the cement slab floor was the final obstacle, so next trip we're in. It may take us a day or two to find and gather up what we want, then we contact our … sponsor. He'll give us our final instructions and then we get a huge paycheck. So, I suggest you find a new place for your precious car soon, or you'll have to leave it behind. But not in here. They could probably trace it back to you, even if it is mostly junkyard parts."

"I suppose I could buy a brand new one. You know some guy bought up all the supplies when DeLorean closed up shop. There were enough parts to make thousands of cars, just sitting in storage. He shipped them all to Texas and builds brand new cars from unused old parts made in the 1980s."

"No, I didn't know. What's more … I don't care. But, if you want this DeLorean so badly, you better move it—tonight would be good. Either way we're gone in a few days … sooner if we get lucky."

"Hey, it's a great car," Cal said, a little defensively.

"Well, I don't care. Let's clean up and get something to eat. Hammering through that concrete floor and skipping lunch doesn't go well with my stomach."

"If you didn't blow off yesterday, we would've been done hours ago."

"Some days you just need to rest," responded Donald. "I'm still sore from months of digging."

"Yeah, ya got that right," came the reply. "After we eat, I'll bring the trailer back. I'm not abandoning this car."

Donald flipped a switch on a box that the electric wire ran through, and the lights in the tunnel went dark. Without further talking, the two dusted off a lot of dirt from their clothing, removed their gloves, and climbed out of the overalls they were wearing. They washed their faces and hands using a bucket full of water that was sitting near a makeshift table by the door.

After drying off, they climbed into some cleaner clothes. On their way to the door, Cal flipped another switch on the box and the whole place went dark—they left the barn.

Whiz and I stayed hunkered down in the pitch-black barn without making any noise until we heard the truck start up and drive away. We could tell when they stopped at the gate, and in a few minutes the truck picked up speed as it headed down Jamestown Road.

"That was a close one," I finally said.

I expected Whiz to answer back with a similar response, but all he did was flip on his flashlight and point it toward the opening of the hole. He ran the beam of light from the hole to the switchbox, following the wire.

"What're you thinking?" I asked, but I think I already knew.

"We need to investigate that hole."

Yeah, that's what I expected.

CHAPTER 8
The Whole Hole

"I think we should get out of here while we have a chance," I said, but Whiz didn't even hear me.

"Those two appear to be up to something no good and we need to find out what."

With a feeling of dread, I turned my flashlight on and pointed it around the barn—hoping not to see anyone. I didn't.

"That'll have to wait," I let out, trying another angle. "I should head home for supper. If we leave now I can still make it in plenty of time. And, I need to get this paint off my face. It's really itchy."

"It will only take a few minutes longer to climb into the hole and find out what this is all about."

I had to admit, I was a little curious myself, so I looked down into the hole. Whiz, however, walked over to the door and looked out through a crack.

"Nobody out there," he announced. "It should be safe enough to take a quick look."

Whiz pointed his flashlight beam back to the electric box and walked over to it. He flipped a large toggle switch, and the barn lit up again. He quickly flipped the switch the other way and the barn went dark again.

"We do not need to broadcast through all the barn cracks that we are in here. Donald and Cal could easily come back."

With just the slightest hesitation, he flipped the other switch and the tunnel lights came on. That didn't make me feel any better. But, we both shut off our flashlights and stashed them in our Surveillance Suit pockets. Whiz began climbing down the ladder—and I couldn't let him do it alone, so I climbed down, too. What did it matter? If we only took a few minutes, I could still be home in time.

At the bottom was a small room—dug out with enough headroom to stand up. Like the hole, the room had reinforced wooden walls and support beams holding up a wooden ceiling. They built this pretty well.

We looked around. There were picks and shovels leaning against one wall. It was otherwise quite empty.

"This is sort of a letdown," I said. "There's nothing here ... just an empty room."

"Cal's yell indicated that they had just finished. So, perhaps they will now start moving down whatever it is they needed an underground room for."

"They seemed to be quite excited over a little hole in the ground." I didn't think this was worth being excited over.

"There must be more to it," said Whiz. "This can't be the whole hole. Cal and Donald talked about breaking through a cement floor. This is just a hole."

Whiz began examining everything in his Sherlock Holmes manner. He ran his fingers over the dirt floor and up the wooden wall. He began tapping the wall with his knuckles.

"What's up, M?"

"There are wheel tracks going into this wall. It also sounds hollow behind this section," he said, as he tapped again.

"A secret door?"

Whiz didn't answer but kept feeling the cracks and support boards. He pulled one brace and a big part of the wall moved.

"Help me with this, K."

I grabbed one side and we pulled about a third of the wall inward and moved it out of the way. We both stared at the opening we revealed—a tunnel!

It was big enough for a person to stoop in and move about comfortably. Just inside was a wheeled cart that they obviously used to move dirt, and a string of lights hung from the ceiling, lighting it as far back as I could see. The thick electric wire stretched along the ground—it was a long tunnel.

Whiz snapped some pictures, as I tried to get my bearings.

"Hey, M,"

"Yes, K?"

"I think this tunnel goes to the west."

"Yes. It definitely goes west."

"That's toward the Air Force Station," I said.

"It certainly is," Whiz replied with a thoughtful look. "Why would they dig a tunnel toward an abandoned place like that?"

Then I realized I hadn't told Whiz about my encounter with Mr. Lovett.

"It's not abandoned."

He turned his thoughtful look to me, and it got even more thoughtful.

"What do you mean?" he asked.

"Mr. Lovett told me all about it. It was a radar station back before there were space cameras and other sensors. He said they decommissioned the radar but that they still do some secret stuff there. A small Air Force team shows up a couple of times a month."

"Agent K," he said in a very businesslike manner. "This changes the whole purpose behind our investigation."

"Well," I said, forgetting about supper. "We got this far ... I suppose we should crawl through the tunnel to see if it goes all the way to the Air Force Station."

"Affirmative, Agent K." I knew he wouldn't put up a fuss.

So, we stooped over and entered the tunnel, heading west, toward the secret base. Whiz entered first, with me close behind—where else would I be? Someone had to watch that brainiac's back. Inside it was quite roomy. I guess if two big guys needed to go in and out a lot, pulling a cart full of dirt, they would make it big enough for themselves and that made it plenty big for me and Whiz—but we still had to stoop a little. The lights were like little Christmas tree lights, but only every ten feet rather than every few inches. It provided plenty of light as we hurried through the tunnel.

"How far are we gonna go?" I had to ask.

"Let us see if we can get to the end. That would give us an indication as to what these guys are up to."

We kept half crawling, half walking—for a long time. Eventually, we did reach the end, where we were able to stand up.

"Wow," Whiz proclaimed, as he looked around.

The far end had a room like the one at the front. We could stand up and walk around, and it also had a hole in the roof with an extension ladder sticking up into it.

"Ah," exclaimed Whiz. "This is the reason for running 240 volts down here."

Whiz was examining a big tank with an air compressor attached, just like the one at Johnson's Garage and Body Shop. Mr. Johnson used it for filling tires, spraying paint, and running other air powered tools. The hose attached to this one connected to what looked like a small jack hammer.

"A chisel to dig a tunnel?" I asked.

"Of course ... they were not removing rocks as we watched," said Whiz, as he pointed his flashlight up the hole in the roof. "They were removing chunks of concrete. There is a concrete slab above us with a sizable hole chipped into it. This is the source of that pounding sound we felt through the ground."

I moved closer, so I could see up as well.

"I wonder what's up there." I shined my flashlight up. "I think I see the underside of a table."

"There is only one irrefutable way to find out, Agent K."

I looked at my watch—then back up the hole.

"Okay, but we gotta be quick. I won't be too late for supper if we hurry."

Whiz was heading up the ladder before I finished talking. I started up after him. Above the hole in the concrete was a small room. We had to crawl out from under a table near the edge of the room. Whiz and I both pointed our flashlight beams around as we looked the place over. It appeared to be a small storage room with shelves along two of the walls. The third wall had the table we crawled under and a couple of chairs, and farther in was the fourth wall, with some boxes and a door.

The shelves had many metal boxes stacked on them. With just the two flashlight beams and the small amount of light coming from the tunnel under the table, it wasn't very easy to make out anything else. I was shining my beam around the door, when I spotted the light switch.

"Whiz, do we dare turn on the light?"

"Definitely not, Agent K," he replied with a very distinct emphasis on my code name.

"Sorry, Agent M."

Before he could say anything else, the room became much darker. My flashlight was still on, and Whiz's was also. But the light under the table had gone off! Then it came back on and just as quickly went out again.

"Oh, man," I gasped. "We're in for it now. They must have come back, and now they know we're in here."

Whiz kept a much calmer head about him. "They may have returned. It is certain that someone turned the lights off, but that does not necessarily mean they know we are here. They may have thought they forgot to turn the lights off when they left."

"Unless they see the wall we moved." I pointed my flashlight around the room. "Well, what do we do?"

"We sit tight, quietly, and listen. If they think someone has found their tunnel, they may try to sneak up on us in the dark. If we do not hear anything, then it is probably safe to return to the barn and escape."

Whiz looked cool, but the slight quiver in his voice let me know that he, too, was a bit scared. We both quietly laid on the floor, stuck our heads into the hole, and listened. With an ominous feeling, I looked at my watch.

"Agent M, if I don't leave now, and really hurry, I'll definitely be late for supper. I may be late anyway if I have to take time to get this awful paint off my face first."

"Perhaps we have waited long enough. We shall see."

He climbed slowly down into the hole, and I followed. We moved as quietly as we could, still listening for any movement at the other end. It was much slower going on the way out. We didn't dare turn on our flashlights, but I estimated we were nearing the end of the tunnel when we could hear talking.

"Okay, now your precious car's loaded on the trailer, so we can concentrate on our job," Donald stated.

About this time, the lights in the tunnel came back on! We were now in what felt like the brightest tunnel ever. Going from pitch-black to a bunch of light bulbs can be painful.

Whiz signaled me to turn around and made some crawling motions. I took the hint and started back toward the Air Force end of the tunnel as fast as I could go without making too much noise. Whiz was right behind me, and I could hear him panting—partly from running stooped over and partly from fear. At least *mine* was partly from fear—okay maybe mostly.

We reached the end and paused to catch our breath before continuing. As we climbed the ladder, the two guys dropped noisily into the tunnel at the other end. We just made it—I hope.

"You didn't close off the tunnel again, Cal," Donald said. "You've been leaving it open a lot recently. Just because we're near the end is no reason to let down on secrecy."

"I did close it. But, don't forget, you left the light on," Cal responded.

We didn't wait for more of the conversation.

"What now, M?" I asked as we crawled into the Air Force storage room.

I was sure to use his code name since we were definitely neck-deep in a mystery case now.

CHAPTER 9
Trespassing and a Robbery

"We must find a good hiding place in the event they come all the way here. Which is inevitable, since I can conceive of no other reason for them to enter the tunnel."

Again, we pointed our flashlights around the room. There were stacks of boxes—some on shelves and some on the floor near the door, with no place to hide anywhere.

"Unless we make ourselves very skinny and squeeze behind some of these boxes, there's nowhere to go." My voice trembled a bit—though I tried to hide it.

"Out the door, K," Whiz commanded, as sure of his decision as ever.

He carefully twisted the door knob, and the latch made a little click as it disengaged. Whiz slowly pulled, and the door opened. It was a tiny bit squeaky but not too loud. I could hear the guys getting closer. They obviously didn't feel the need to be quiet. That helped, since it would be harder for them to hear us—the louder, the better. We went through the door and shut it softly.

We were now in a hallway with several doors on either side. Some doors had little rectangular windows like the doors at school, but most were solid. At one end, the hallway opened into a large room—that's where we headed. The room had several desks and looked kinda like a normal office, not too different from where my dad works—except his office is part of a big garage building where they store all the town trucks and equipment. There were computer monitors, keyboards, and telephones—the kind with many buttons on them. This place sure didn't look abandoned from the inside. But we needed a place to hide, so we frantically pointed our flashlights around and into every corner.

"M," I said, as I lit up three filing cabinets along the front wall. "We might be able to squeeze behind those."

"Good eye, K," he responded. "We will need to make more space. If we are quiet, we may be able to move them farther from the wall without it looking conspicuous."

There was already some space behind them, but we teamed up, pulling on the locked drawer handles, and made enough space behind them while keeping them even with each other. We had just managed to climb into our hiding spot and switch off our flashlights, when the door to the storeroom opened.

Through the crack between two of the filing cabinets I could make out the shadow of one of the guys as he made his way down the hallway toward us. They had turned on the overhead light in the storeroom, and it provided a lot of brightness to the otherwise dark hallway—especially with our eyes accustomed to the blackness. Whiz was sticking his head above mine so he, too, could make out the scene in the hallway. In a few seconds, the second guy came into view.

"Okay, which room do we want?"

"I dunno. We need to look in all of them. I was given a description of the safe, but nothing more."

"What if there's more than one?"

"We take 'em all."

The door to the storeroom closed, so no light got into the hall until one of them flipped the hallway light switch on, and the whole place got very bright. I almost jumped at the sudden shock of so much light, but I managed to keep calm, and so did Whiz. The guy stuck his head in the front office, gave a quick look, then turned and walked back down the hallway. They both were opening doors and entering each room as they went until one guy called out.

"Donald! This must be the one. It looks like a NASA launch center in here."

The other guy came out of the room he was in and raced to the end of the hallway where the first guy was calling. The door automatically shut behind them. I took a breath then—but, I wouldn't swear to it.

"Now is our chance to leave, Agent K," said Whiz, in a halting voice that sounded like his throat had as big a lump in it as mine.

I wasn't going to argue with that logic, and I managed to say, "Okay," but nothing more.

We climbed out from behind the cabinets and tiptoed toward the hallway. We couldn't hear anything from the room at the end. Then, I took a good look down the hallway. There were several closed doors on each side. It only then dawned on me that I was so busy looking for a place to hide—and it was dark—that I didn't pay any attention to which room we came out of.

"Which door?" I asked.

Whiz didn't answer but kept walking, so, of course, I just followed. He walked quietly, straight to one of the doors and opened it. There was a light on inside this room, so it must be the storage room. We went in.

"We're gonna need the cart. Go get it," one of them said. "And the rope and pulley. I'll look around some more to make sure we found the right one ... or the only one."

The voice was loud enough that the guy must have been in the hallway, and since the cart was in the tunnel, he must be coming this way.

"Hide," Whiz whispered to me as he pushed me toward boxes sitting on the floor.

I climbed behind them—pushing them away from the wall, as I scrunched down. Whiz pushed in right behind me which pushed the boxes a little more. But, if the guy went straight to the tunnel he might not see us. It was our only hope.

Within seconds after we settled in, the door opened, and the guy came into the storeroom. He went straight to the table, but rather than ducking under and climbing into the tunnel, he pulled the table out of the way and gave it a push toward us—it toppled over, but he didn't look back. He went straight down the ladder backwards, and we could hear him shuffling off down the tunnel.

"What do we do now, Whiz?" I asked, with a giant lump in my throat.

"Shhh, Agent K," he replied in a whisper. "We have no knowledge of the second guy's location. He may be within earshot."

"Well, should we head down the tunnel?" I whispered just as quietly.

"Definitely not. If that guy is going after the cart we saw at the tunnel entrance, we would not be able to maneuver around him to get out. We must assume he will be heading back this way very shortly."

"Then we have to get outta here."

"I suggest we head back to the office and resume our position behind the filing cabinets."

We crawled out from behind the box and moved as quietly as we dared. I opened the door slowly, trying not to let it squeak, as Whiz looked out to see if there was any movement from the other guy.

"Onward, K," he whispered.

I pulled the door farther and we headed through, into the hallway. I let it close even slower, so it wouldn't make any noise. Then, my heart stopped beating—I think—because, as soon as I let go of the door knob, the door between us and the office opened.

There was nowhere to go so, as if by instinct, Whiz and I together pushed against the wall—I was trying to do some Indian mystic trick of melting into the wall but it didn't work. The guy came out of the room but he headed toward the office without looking back. We were goners now! We couldn't go back into the storage room and one of the bad guys was between us and our hiding spot.

Whiz moved his head to look at each door in the hallway, and with a simple handwave to me, he slinked over and entered the room directly across. I followed him in and closed the door as fast as I could while looking through the window hoping the guy wouldn't return. As the door lock clicked, my heart started beating again—until, a few minutes later, the other guy's voice sounded from the storage room.

"Hey, Donald, come help with this. It's heavy."

The guy, Donald, came noisily down the hallway and into the storage room across from us.

"Should we make a run for the office, while they're busy in the storage room?" I asked.

"That would not be wise. We have no way of knowing how long it will take them to get the cart out of the hole. They could reenter the hallway at any time."

We quickly found hiding spots behind the many worktables and cabinets scattered around the room.

The noise as they pulled the cart out of the hole echoed through the quiet building. On the other hand, we stayed as quiet as we could. We said nothing more, as we waited. Whiz, however, shined his flashlight around the room, examining all the strange looking equipment.

Soon, they pulled the cart through the storage room door. The noisy wheels trailed off down the hall. Then, we heard heavy things being manhandled in the back room. Eventually, they pulled the cart back down the hall, but it had a much deeper and muted sound. There must be something quite heavy on it. They huffed and puffed and grumbled a lot as they tugged it along.

Then everything got quiet.

"Do you think they're in the tunnel?" I asked.

"That is quite doubtful. It would take more time to lower something that heavy into the hole in the floor. But, perhaps a quick look is called for."

"What? No," I exclaimed. "If they look over and see us through the window, we're doomed."

"Relax, K."

And Whiz slowly stood up and moved his head so he could see across the hallway through the window. He stooped back down just as quickly.

"They are most assuredly not gone yet. The cart is in the middle of the doorway with a big filing cabinet on it."

"A filing cabinet? I thought they were stealing a safe."

"It is a safe. But, it is the size and shape of the filing cabinets we were hiding behind in the office. It looks much more substantial, though, and it has a dial on one of the drawers."

The noise started again. There was a lot of grunting and banging. It sounded like they were tearing apart the ceiling or wall.

"Now attach the pulley to that beam. It's gotta be tight. This thing's heavy."

"Okay, let's get the safe over here and wrap the rope around it."

"It's not going to be easy," Cal complained.

"Just do it," came the reply. "And be careful. There's some delicate electronic stuff in here along with a whole bunch of data."

"What kind of data?"

"Something top secret is all he would tell me."

"Who?"

"The guy who hired us. I've told you all I know about him … which isn't much."

More grunting noises came and then there was a big thud as if they dropped the cart into the hole.

"Well, that does it," Donald said. "Now jump down so you can guide the safe as I lower it. Get it to lay on its side or it'll never get through the tunnel."

After some more bangs and a loud "ouch," it quieted down and Donald came back into the hallway. Whiz and I hunkered down and held our breaths.

Donald went down the hallway, and the light switch clicked off in the far room. He walked back up the hallway and the hallway light switch made a similar sounding click. The room got extremely dark as the light coming through the window went out. Footsteps sounded again as he opened the storage room door. Seconds later, the door closed.

Whiz and I were now alone in the very dark room of the secret Air Force building! I let a moment or two pass before I spoke.

"What now, Whiz? You realize how late I am for supper?"

"We must ensure our way is clear, then we may traverse the tunnel to the barn for our getaway. Sorry about your supper, but I also am late." He didn't even correct my use of his name during a case.

"Let's see where they are, Agent M." I used his code name to show I still could be professional under these circumstances.

"A wise move, Agent K," he responded.

With the lights out, and no outside windows, this place was as dark as anywhere I've ever been. Whiz was feeling his way along the workbenches, and I was holding on to his Surveillance Suit.

Being blind allowed my other senses to perform better, which wasn't always a good thing. The itchy feeling in my face was getting downright annoying. The dry paint was crinkling with every movement of my cheeks and eyebrows. It hurt a bit as it pulled the skin, but I kept holding on to Whiz as he slowly made his way to the door and out.

I could tell when we got to the hallway because the sound around me changed. Carefully, or so I thought, I reached out for the wall with my left hand as we crossed to the storage room door. Not being able to see, I jammed my fingers into the doorframe, letting out a little yelp.

"Quiet, K," Whiz admonished. "We do not know for sure that Donald and Cal have completely gone."

"Sorry," I whispered, but I sure didn't feel sorry—my fingers hurt.

Whiz paused, then slowly turned the knob. As it unlatched, he gently, and very slowly, pushed it open. I could see light from the tunnel. It was good to see again but that meant the bad guys were probably still in there.

CHAPTER 10

Trapped!

We entered the room, and Whiz reversed his slow-motion action with the door, closing it. The table that used to be over the hole was still on its side and out of the way. I could see the pulley system that they left over the hole. They tore through the ceiling and wrapped a thick rope around a steel beam in the roof.

I dropped to my knees, then to my belly, as I edged over to the opening—Whiz followed.

"I can hear them," I told Whiz as he crawled up.

"It will take them as long to get the safe out at the other end as it took to put it in at this end … maybe longer. We may be in for quite a wait."

"Jeez, that's all I need. I'm already late, and it's only getting later. And, my face itches!"

"I suggest we climb down into the tunnel to save a little bit of time," Whiz answered. "Since they turned out the lights in this room, it is safe to deduce that they do not intend to return. Therefore, as long as we are quiet and stay far enough back that we are unseen, we can be ready to make our exit at the earliest possible moment."

"I guess," I replied, but I wasn't sure I wanted to get that close to them. Then, I thought a little more. "What if they come back for the ladder?"

"It is a lightweight extension ladder. If they were at all concerned about keeping it, they could easily have set it on top of the cart with the safe. It would not have added any real weight or otherwise hampered their escape. They probably intended to leave it behind. They appear to be abandoning the air compressor and tools, also. The cost of pulling off a very lucrative crime."

That was well reasoned, I thought. "Okay, let's go."

I climbed down first, and Whiz was right behind. I felt for my flashlight just to make sure I was ready when the lights went out again. I'm sure they would turn them out as they left the barn.

Down in the tunnel, the noise from the other end was louder. The tunnel focused all the ruckus straight at us. But, we continued toward the barn.

"That safe must be quite heavy, K. Look at the depth of the marks left by the cart wheels. We now know why they made the tunnel as tall and wide as they did. They must have known how big the safe would be."

I looked at the tracks, but I didn't answer. My heart was beating as fast as I've ever felt it, and there was a giant lump in my throat. I wanted to run fast in the opposite direction. But, that wasn't an option. We kept moving toward the danger zone.

"The rope's hooked. Come up and help from this end." The one I thought was Donald yelled.

His voice was much louder than I felt comfortable with, signaling we were too close, so I stopped. Whiz stopped, too. Neither one of us spoke. There was some noise that sounded like one of them climbing up the ladder and then some grunting.

"Pull!" Donald commanded.

"I am!" Cal responded.

More grunting.

"Now push. Hard!" Donald yelled. "As it swings away from the hole, I'll let it drop."

A loud thud signaled the safe hitting the ground.

"Now change the pulley so we can lift it over the truck," Donald yelled, again.

"Release more rope," Cal replied.

Whiz and I relaxed a bit as we heard them moving around up in the barn. Soon, they were pulling again and we heard the creaking of wood. They must be lifting the safe.

"I am not sure those beams in the old barn can take much weight," Whiz whispered, over my shoulder.

I said nothing, but I heard an engine start, and it groaned as the truck moved. Soon, there was another, gentler, thud as the safe must have been lowered onto the truck bed.

"Tie it down tightly, Cal, so it doesn't slide while we're driving."

"Seriously? That thing's too heavy to move around."

"Just tie it!" came the harsh reply.

Another thud and the sound of the guys jumping out of the truck came rolling into the tunnel.

Whiz and I instinctively moved back a little and pressed up against the dirt wall.

"Hook the trailer to the hitch and let's roll," Donald said.

The noise of the truck moving around again came down into the tunnel, and soon, the lights went out, and our wait was over. We were once again in the pitchest black there is. The truck rumbled as it left the barn and the barn door closed loudly soon afterward.

"Now is our chance to exit this dusty confinement, Agent K."

"Let's go," I agreed.

We hurried to the end of the tunnel, but with only our flashlights to ease the darkness, and while trying to be very quiet, it was slow moving. We did finally get to the end where we stopped and listened. Nothing.

They didn't replace the wall that hid the tunnel from the underground room. I guessed they had their loot and were making their escape. No sense in hiding anything—they weren't coming back.

"They should be gone. I think it is safe to remove ourselves from this hole." Whiz then turned on his flashlight.

I once again followed closely behind as Whiz led the way to the ladder. He climbed up first, with me right behind. It was still quite dark, but it felt great to be out of the hole. Now, our only problem was bulls!

Whiz shined his flashlight around the barn. The car was gone, and there were lots of tire tracks from the truck. I flipped my flashlight on and looked at all the dirt piles filling up most of the free space.

"Hey, Donald," Cal yelled from outside. "Did you leave the light on? There's a light on in the barn."

Oh man, were we in trouble now! As if we practiced, Whiz and I both turned our flashlights off at the same time.

"Hide," Whiz whispered.

The sound of movement came from his direction, so he must have already been doing that. I climbed over one of the dirt piles and hunkered down to hide behind the peak. The noise from our movement had died down as the guy managed to get the lock off the door. I could hear the latch coming up as the other guy came stomping over. Then, the big door creaked open.

"I don't see any light. I knew I turned it off," said Donald.

"I saw a light. And, you left the tunnel light on when we went to eat," replied Cal.

"I did not. I don't know why the light was on, but I turned it off. And, there's no light on now."

"I saw a light. It was moving around like a swinging bulb."

"Why would the light bulb be swinging around? There's no wind in here."

"Maybe ..." he paused. "Maybe it was a flashlight being waved around. Someone's in here. Whoever it was turned on the lights and moved the wall away from the tunnel entrance."

"You're imaging things ... that's called paranoia, Cal. There's nobody here and there's nobody in the Air Force building. Besides that ... we got what we wanted and we'll never be back. What do we care if a light was on? In two weeks, the Air Force will know about the break-in and be all over this place."

"I suppose you're right. Let's get out of here, I'm starting to get the creeps," said Cal.

The CREEPS? He's starting to get them? I've been sitting here on top of a dirt pile trying not to breathe, and trying not to move, even though my left leg was falling asleep.

"Turn the lights on and we'll take a quick look first," Donald said. "Just in case."

And almost immediately the barn got bright. That's when I made a mistake. The light startled me and I tried to hunker down even more. That movement started a small avalanche of soil flowing down the side of my dirt pile. It wasn't really very much, or very loud, but in the quiet barn it was like an explosion.

"Who's there!" Donald yelled, as he started to climb up toward me.

Then, there was big bang from behind him. Whiz had apparently seen what was going on from his hiding spot and threw a clod of dirt against the far barn wall as a distraction. It worked—just like with the bull. They both stopped and turned toward the noise. This allowed me time to slide down the far side of the hill.

My noise, though, had reattracted their attention. I could hear one of them coming back up the hill—it was Donald. By this time, I was in a little valley between the piles and had circled around toward Whiz who was at the far side of the hole—he also had a guy chasing him.

And here was where some really weird stuff began.

Everything was in slow motion. The motion didn't really slow down, my brain just began working extra fast—kinda like Whiz's does all the time, I guess. I could see Donald coming out from around the dirt piles where I had been, and beyond the hole was Whiz, moving away from Cal, who was chasing him, but like I said, it was all in slow motion. I was running too, I think, but not getting very far.

I headed toward the barn door, but many things were racing through my head—the door, the bulls, the distance to the road, where my bike was, how dark it was outside. They shut the door when they came in, and I could see the latch was down. I mentally computed how long it would take me to lift the latch and came to the disheartening conclusion that Donald would grab me before I could lift it even halfway. I also thought about the bulls outside in the pasture and how the commotion must have aroused them. They were probably waiting just outside the door. I still didn't know how fast they could run.

Once outside, if I could make it, I needed to run to the road. Was I faster than Donald? Should I turn right at the road and try to get my bike or should I turn left and try to run all the way back to Jasper Springs? What about Whiz? Could he outrun Cal? If not, how could I help while Donald was still on me. All this went through my head as I was turning to take a step toward the barn door.

Halfway through this step, I turned my head the other way and could see that the wall, with the missing slats we crawled in through, was even farther from me. Cal was blocking Whiz's path to the missing slats. As options sped through my brain, I began nudging my leg away from the barn door. My body twisted, on its own, because I sure wasn't in much control, and as my right foot hit the ground, I made a 'fake and turn' that Coach Stapleton would have given me a medal for.

My body ducked—again, on its own—and I could see Donald lunging toward me, but he had taken aim before I changed direction, so he was too high and too far to the side. By the time he arrived, I was a step to his left, and he went sailing around me.

Without consciously thinking it, I yelled, "Tunnel!" and could see Whiz had the same idea.

CHAPTER 11

Tunnel Escape

My body started moving faster, or at least my thoughts were coming at a more normal speed. So, everything looked faster. As I made a few steps toward the hole, Whiz had already arrived. He jumped down the hole without using the ladder, but Cal was closing in.

Once again, my body, acting without my knowledge, pushed off hard and leaped toward Cal. I turned and hit him with my feet in the middle of his chest. He went down hard, and I also landed hard—right in front of the hole. I pulled myself across the few feet to the ladder and used it to pull myself, rather than climbing, down into the hole.

At the bottom, Whiz was standing up and holding the ladder, and as I came down, he pulled on the rope to allow the extension to drop. The ladder was now a good five feet below the top of the hole.

"That should slow them down a little, Joey. Run."

I was a little startled by Whiz's use of my name, but my mind was still running fast enough to know that now was not the time to discuss standard Tanner-Dent Agency procedures. I ducked down into the tunnel and moved as fast as I could behind Whiz.

We had only made it about a quarter of the way to the Air Force building when the lights went out. This caused Whiz to trip, and of course, I fell right over him. Amazingly, we both still had flashlights in our hands, and without a word between us, we got up and moved off—with very little light and at a much slower pace.

Soon we could hear the men following. They must have made it into the hole by jumping the way Whiz did. That was a good drop. Of course, the darkness hampered them as much, or even more, than us—we, at least, had flashlights.

When we reached the cavern under the Air Force storage room, we quickly climbed up the ladder. First Whiz, and then me.

"Pull the ladder up," Whiz commanded, and I stashed my flashlight in a pocket and helped him get the ladder out of the hole.

Since we had been in the room a couple of times already, I knew where the door was without getting the flashlight out of my pocket. I opened it, and we both went clumsily into the hallway.

"Where to now, M?" I asked. "Should we hide in one of these other rooms or go back to the front office?"

"I think our best option is to resume our former position in the office," Whiz answered. "That has served us well, and it is near the only building exit I am aware of."

"You think we need to go outside?"

"The building is not that large and only has the one hallway. If these guys make it up the hole, it is only a matter time before they find us."

"Jeez ... I was hoping we only had to wait until they got tired of looking for us. You think they can get out of the hole without the ladder?"

"With the air compressor as a base and one guy on the other's shoulders, it may be quite possible for one guy to extricate himself from the hole."

Boy, even under this stress, Whiz can bring out a Whiz Word. "What's extricate?"

"It means to remove from or get out of something. You know, you do have a dictionary sitting on the desk in your bedroom. I have seen it with my own eyes."

"Okay, enough with the lecture. What's our plan? To stay here or go outside?"

"I would recommend that we stay here until such time as they get out of the hole. It would take a little time, but the real question is how much time can they afford to spend looking for us? They do have the loot they were after and are in the middle of their getaway."

Our conversation came to a quick end as we heard them at the bottom of the hole. They weren't too happy and were arguing with each other—mostly about why they didn't leave the lights on. We got our flashlights out and made our way to the front office.

I started toward our old hiding place but Whiz pointed his flashlight around the room, examining everything. The guy never stopped.

"Joey ... now you have me doing it." He paused for a moment and took a deep breath as if to relax. Then, he continued. "Agent K, if this is not an abandoned station—and by the looks of it, it is most definitely not—those telephones should be in working order. I suggest we call the authorities."

"Then, go for it," I agreed, with the first feeling of relief I've had all night.

He went over to the closest desk and picked up the receiver.

"I have a dial tone," he said.

I smiled. He punched in the number for the Jasper Springs Police and waited. The voice on the other end was loud enough for me to hear, and it didn't sound good.

"The number cannot be completed as dialed," Whiz repeated.

He tried again. Same result. He dialed 911. Nothing.

"We must need an access code to make a call from this system."

He put the receiver back in the phone cradle and brought over two pads of paper from the desk with a couple of pens. He handed me one set.

"What's this for?"

"We cannot inform the authorities, so we must document what we know, Agent K. We did not get a very lengthy look at the two perpetrators, but write down everything you can remember about them ... mention Cal's fascination with his DeLorean automobile."

"Why? Shouldn't we be using our time to escape?"

"Our options for escape are quite limited. This area is surrounded by a high fence with razor wire at the top and that assumes we can actually get out the front door. We do not know if the locking mechanism prevents it from opening from both sides. There may be a padlock on the outside, and this building has no windows."

"Then we need to look for a better hiding spot."

"What we must do is leave behind the best clues we can to enable the police or the Air Force to track down and capture these two thieves in the event they get to us."

Well, that scared me again—but, I guess, not enough to make everything go into slow motion.

I pointed my flashlight at the page and was about to begin when Whiz stood up and dropped his paper on the chair.

"We need a photograph!" he blurted out.

"Of what?" I had to ask, knowing I didn't want to hear the answer.

He pulled his digital camera out of one of the pockets he had sewn into his Surveillance Suit.

"We need a picture of Donald and Cal."

"And just how are you going to get that?" Again, I didn't want to hear the answer.

"Follow me," was his only response.

I set my pad down and followed. We entered the storage room very quietly. The two were still at the bottom of the hole, and by the grunting and other noises, it seemed they were trying to climb out just like Whiz suggested. We crawled carefully over to the hole. Whiz stuck the camera over it and pressed the shutter button. There was a bright flash that blinded us for a split second, but the commotion from below was even more dramatic.

There was a big crash from the hole. My guess is that Donald and Cal were even more surprised and blinded by the flash. Whiz snapped another picture.

"Get the ladder," yelled Donald. "And turn the lights on. Hurry!"

We quietly backed out of the room, but why we were quiet was a mystery to me. They obviously knew we were there. Whiz followed me to the office.

"Quickly, Agent K. We must document what we know and there is no time to waste."

"Right, M," I answered, without any idea what I was going to write.

What do you leave behind when you know you're about to be killed? I started anyway. I had about a half a page of stuff about the car and what little I could remember about the two guys—not much other than their first names. About the time I finished, my heart got another jolt. Cal must have gotten to the other end because the lights in the tunnel flashed on. Through the open storage room door, the dim glow of light gave an eerie appearance to the otherwise dark office.

"We must hurry," said Whiz. "They should have the ladder here in just a few minutes."

Whiz continued writing furiously and completed his third page, when he finally stopped.

There was a new noise coming from the storage room—the clanking of what had to be the ladder as Donald and Cal were sticking it up through the opening in the floor.

"We should get out of here … now!" I panicked.

Hoping they would decide to escape with their loot rather than fool with us was not working for me right now.

"It is time to try the front door," responded Whiz, a little more calmly than I thought was called for, but I wasn't going to argue—it was our only path to freedom.

I handed my pad to Whiz, and he put them both down near the edge of one of the desks, as we made our way to the door. Being the first one there, I put my hand on the bar running across it and pushed. The locking mechanism clicked, but nothing else happened.

"There is a cypher lock just above the bar. Twist that knob first," said Whiz.

"What's a cypher ..." I started to ask, when I decided that now was not the time to discuss a Whiz Word.

I moved my flashlight beam up and saw a small box with a little round knob. I twisted it and heard a click. While holding the knob from turning back, I pushed on the bar again, and the door gave way— opening out to a small cement slab.

Whiz was right behind me as I left the building. We ran out onto a parking area and looked around for our next move. Aside from our flashlights, we had some light from the moon which had risen a little. The few remaining leaves on the trees lining the western edge of Farmer Zimmer's field blocked some of that light, and there were thin clouds filtering much of its shine.

"Agent K, we should move into the tall weeds well off the pavement."

"Righto," I exclaimed, and headed toward the side of the building in the direction of the road.

"Dive," Whiz called softly, when we were about fifteen feet into the weeds.

I dove down and flattened as much as I could against the ground. Whiz was beside me. Then, the door burst open, and the two guys came rushing out.

CHAPTER 12
Bad Guys, Top Secrets, Bulls—A Choice?

"Block the door with something so it doesn't close," yelled Donald. "The last thing we need is for that door to lock us out."

"I got it," Cal responded.

"Hey, you kids," yelled Donald. "You better come with us now or you'll be in big trouble. You're trespassing on a military installation. Turn yourselves in and we can go easy on you. Otherwise, the Air Force will lock you away in one of their secret jails and you'll never get out."

I didn't know what kind of secret jails the Air Force had, but I was willing to take my chances with them rather than these two thieves. Whiz wasn't moving either, so I think he was with me on that. We kept watching, as they looked around the open field in the dim moonlight.

They moved to the edge of the pavement and walked around the perimeter. My breath stopped as they stared in our direction. I'll have to give Whiz a big ol' thanks for the Surveillance Suits—they worked.

Donald and Cal stopped very close to us but didn't leave the pavement. They got quiet and listened. They surely didn't hear any noise from me. After one last look, Donald turned away.

"Let's circle the building. You go that way," Donald pointed. "They can't be far … they were only a few steps ahead of us getting outta the door."

The two walked in different directions and were soon out of sight. Only a few moments passed, when they reappeared together in front of the building.

"You know," Donald said. "That door was alarmed. That was the reason we dug the tunnel instead of cutting through the fence and breaking in."

"I don't hear anything," Cal replied.

"No, but I'm sure there is a bell going off loudly in some Air Force watch room somewhere. We should probably scram … and fast. I don't know how far away they are, but they should be here soon and these kids aren't that important."

They both moved quickly to the front door and rushed into the building.

I poked Whiz with my finger. "Whiz, you suppose the Air Force is on their way to arrest us?"

"Now is not the time to panic, Agent K," he replied. "We can hope that the authorities will assess the situation before shooting at trespassers. But, to be on the safe side, we should reenter the building and escape through the tunnel ourselves as soon as it is clear."

"Okay, M," I responded, and we both got up and slunk toward the door.

The brick they used to keep the door open was still in place. Whiz carefully opened it, and I kicked the brick out of the way. We entered very quietly and could hear some ruckus from the storage room—it sounded like the two guys were well into the tunnel and moving quickly. Whiz let the door shut and we made our way to the tunnel.

As we got to the storeroom, I could see that the ladder was gone—and then the lights went out. What else could go wrong today—or was it tomorrow, yet?

"The perpetrators have exited the far end of the tunnel," said Whiz. "We will have to proceed in the dark."

"But what if they're waiting for us? They could ambush us in the dark, and we wouldn't know it."

"A good point," Whiz responded. "But, I think they will be more concerned with getting as far away as possible before the Air Force or police show up."

I had to admit he was probably right, but we still moved slowly and as quietly as we could. We knelt by the hole and pointed our flashlights into it. The big air compressor was now under the opening.

"Agent M," I used Whiz's code name to let him know I was one hundred percent in professional detective mode right now. "They took the ladder ... and jumping down with that machine in the way looks pretty dangerous to me."

"Your assessment is correct, however that does not pose a problem for us."

"Why not?"

"We have a ladder."

"They took the ladder …" As the words were coming out of my mouth, I remembered, we had pulled up the other ladder.

Whiz pointed his flashlight at the ladder on the floor to emphasize this fact. I couldn't see his face, but I'm sure it had one of his usual expressions of disappointment.

Without further discussion, we moved the ladder back to the hole and lowered it. It made some noise but we did our best to keep quiet. After steadying it, I climbed down with Whiz following close behind.

At the bottom, I stood and pointed my flashlight at the tunnel opening heading toward Farmer Zimmer's barn. It was our only way out, and it was dark. I wasn't too anxious to go in. Whiz stood beside me, and it seemed he felt the same way.

"Well, Agent M," I said, with a slight hesitation in my voice. "I guess we should crawl out."

I pointed my flashlight at my watch. I was over three hours late for supper—in fact it was well past my bedtime and on a school night. That also added to my hesitation, since I would be facing Dad when I got home.

"We are both quite tardy, Agent K. But, we must report this crime as soon as possible."

With that, we ducked our heads and entered the tunnel. We walked quickly, but quietly, and were especially quiet as we neared the end. I kept fearing that Donald and Cal would be at the end waiting for us—in the dark.

Eventually, we arrived at the barn end of the tunnel. We both lit up the underground room with our flashlights. I was quite disheartened by what I saw—or should I say, what I didn't see.

"They took the ladder, Whiz," I exclaimed.

Whiz didn't even call me on not using his code name. He just pointed his flashlight around as if taking in all the fine details. But, the big detail was that there was no ladder for us to climb out of the hole.

"I guess we need to go back and get the other ladder," I said. "We should have brought it with us."

"Planning ahead would have been the appropriate thing to have done and we need to remember that for next time," he kept looking around as he talked.

"Next time? I don't want a next time. I wasn't hot on this time." I stooped down and started back into the tunnel to get the ladder.

"That will not be necessary, Agent K," Whiz responded, as he gave a little tug on my Surveillance Suit. "We will climb up this electric wire."

"What?" I cried, a little loudly.

"This is a heavy-duty cable. Assuming they attached it well enough at the other end, it should suffice to hold our weight. It only needs to hold one at a time."

He grabbed the cable with both hands and pulled down gently. It started to move but after about a foot it stopped. He pulled harder and then pulled himself off the ground a few inches.

"Shine the flashlight ahead of me so I can see the wire," he commanded, and I obeyed.

Hand over hand, he pulled himself up, using his legs as best he could against the wooden sides. It looked a bit awkward, but he kept moving up. Soon, he was at the top and crawled over the edge. He was out.

"Now your turn. I'll light the wire as you come up."

"Well, now that you're up, just turn on the lights, and I'll see everything."

"That would not be a wise course of action, K," he replied.

"Why not? Those guys must be miles away by now. They'd never see the light."

"I am not concerned with the light. The 240 volts of electricity is what bothers me. If the cable were to break or fray, it would probably electrocute you. As long as the power is off, the wire is safe."

"Oh ..." That didn't make me feel any safer.

"Come on up, K. We are wasting time."

I started climbing. I took a bit longer than Whiz, but I wanted to be as careful as possible—or even more careful. I know that being more careful than possible is not possible, but I tried.

At the top, as I crawled over the edge, Whiz helped me to my feet. He aimed his flashlight around the barn, and it seemed to be quite empty. Just like earlier—no bad guys and no car. But the emptiness didn't make me feel any better.

We slowly made our way to the door and both looked through cracks. The moon had risen above the trees enough to give a little light to the field. There was nothing between us and the gate—not even bulls.

BULLS!

After all that, we still had to contend with bulls.

"Where do you think the bulls are, Agent M?" I asked nervously.

"I would have hoped they would be sleeping, but with all the commotion tonight, I do not think that is a reality. In fact," he said, after a short pause. "I see the big one walking toward us."

Whiz also lifted the latch and gave a little push and pull to the barn door.

"We must exit the way we entered. They locked the door from the outside."

I turned and made my way to the back of the barn and climbed over the hay bales to the broken boards that we crawled in through. Whiz was right behind me as I stuck my head out to look for the other bulls.

"I don't see anything." Was that good or bad?

"Let me take a look," Whiz replied.

He pushed up beside me and stuck his head out—with the same result.

"No sign of the other three bulls. Time for our escape."

He climbed out and hunkered down beside the barn as I made my way out. We both stood up against the barn wall as we took a better look around for the bulls.

It seemed to be clear so we began walking carefully and slowly toward the trees at the edge of the field—where we came in. That's when I noticed the cars.

"Whiz," I exclaimed. "Look over there."

I pointed through the trees at the front gate of the Air Force Station. We stopped walking and hunkered down to take notice of the situation.

In front of the gate, three cars with no lights pulled to a stop—many guys were slowly getting out of all three cars. Our escape path was in that direction. I looked back at Farmer Zimmer's gate to gauge how far it was and where the bull was. It was far, and the bull was between us and it.

Whiz likewise, was turning his head between the gate and the woods. He noticed the same thing. And then, it got worse!

CHAPTER 13
Rescued, Finally

Two cars pulled up to Farmer Zimmer's gate and more guys got out. These cars looked like police cars, each with a light rack on the top, but no lights were on—not even headlights. Our goose was cooked.

"Belly down, Agent K," Whiz commanded, and I obeyed, but I felt the need to respond.

"Don't you think it's a bit much to use our code names? We are in something way over our heads, Whiz. This is no longer just a detective case we're on."

"That is precisely what we are on. Donald and Cal, and possibly others, have committed a crime, and we are the only witnesses. This is a perfect case for Tanner-Dent, and we must see this through to the end. The first order of business is to ascertain which side these guys are on. Some appear to be Jasper Springs Police ... we must be sure."

I admit, I was a little bit scared. The 'through to the end' part had me worried, but I just nodded and followed Whiz's lead.

We both lay down as flat as we could and watched. It was harder to see the guys on the Air Force side due to the trees, but we had an unobstructed view of the guys now walking toward the barn. It was dark, but I swear I recognized the silhouette of one of them—I think it was Officer Van Dyke.

I turned back to the Air Force Station and saw through the trees that two guys had reached the building. There was some shouting that I couldn't make out and then the rest of them started running.

On our side of the big fence, the gate opened and one car came in. Three guys—they looked like cops to me—were walking beside the car keeping it between them and the bull. They halted, as they too heard the shouting. One of them, the one I think was Officer Van Dyke, turned his head toward the radio microphone on his right shoulder and started talking. I couldn't make out what he was saying, but he kept following the car as it circled around the bull and up to the barn. We couldn't see the barn door from our angle, so we didn't witness anything more. Except, the other bulls showed up.

On the Air Force side, two of the cars entered the field and were shining very bright spotlights everywhere. It almost looked like daytime over there. Two guys were running along the fence line, shining their flashlights on the fence. I guess they were looking for holes. Several minutes passed with nothing else visible happening.

"They must have found the tunnel by now," Whiz exclaimed.

"Shouldn't we turn ourselves in to the cops or at least make our escape while they're busy inside … and while the bulls are also busy?"

I could see Whiz looking toward our bikes and then back and forth between the Air Force building and barn. The gears were turning in his head, but I sure didn't know what he was thinking—until he spoke.

"I am confident that they know a crime has been committed and being caught trespassing in the middle of it would not go well in our favor. I suggest we leave the pasture and make contact with the authorities by the road. That will at least provide us the opportunity to explain ourselves."

But, just as Whiz seemed to make up his mind, I heard more yelling. Someone was calling—calling our names.

"Whiz! Joey!" The shouts came from two directions.

We heard our names shouted from inside the barn and it sounded like Officer Van Dyke. We also heard our names from the direction of the Air Force building.

"We're in trouble now," I said. "They know it's us. So much for sneaking out."

We could see light coming through the cracks in the barn wall. They found the light switch.

"Whiz! Joey!" the shouting got louder as Officer Van Dyke came out of the barn.

"We've got to give ourselves up," I said quietly in Whiz's ear.

"I agree."

Officer Van Dyke ran to the police car that was herding the bulls away from the barn. That's when Whiz stood up.

"Over here, Officer Van Dyke!" he called.

I stood up too, as Officer Van Dyke turned and pointed a very bright flashlight on us.

"Whiz? Joey?" he called, a little less frantically. "Are you guys okay?"

We assured him we were, as we walked up to him.

He pointed his flashlight at us and a laugh burst out of his mouth. The laugh quickly turned into a frown.

"What are you two doing out here?"

"Would it not be appropriate to get into the safety of the barn as we discuss our excursion?" Whiz responded, as he pointed to the bulls who were taking an interest in us.

"Let's go," Officer Van Dyke said, and we followed him into the barn.

The barn was empty but the ladder was now sticking out of the hole and we could hear the other two cops in the tunnel. They stopped to talk with the Air Force guys coming the other way. The increasing volume of their voices told me they were heading toward us. Soon, the two cops, with their guns drawn, and three guys in Air Force uniforms, with big machine guns, had climbed out of the hole and were looking in amazement at the piles of dirt filling up the barn.

One of them, with a whole bunch of stripes on his arm, began looking closely at me and Whiz.

"These the kids?" he asked. His smile almost broke into a laugh. "I'm Chief Master Sergeant Washington, and I must say, your camouflage gear may be better than mine."

"Yes," Officer Van Dyke replied, also stifling a laugh. "This is Joey Dent and Whiz Tanner." He pointed at each of us.

Their noticing our Surveillance Suits made me a little self-conscious, and the itching on my face got worse. I tried scratching and peeling it away with only a small amount of success.

"I read the notes you left. You've got some story to tell and I want to hear it all." He then turned to Officer Van Dyke. "So, no sign of the guys on this end?"

"Footprints and tire tracks are the only things left here. We've tried not to disturb them. We can dust for fingerprints but there are not a lot of good surfaces for prints. Also, I'd be willing to bet that they were wearing workman's gloves most of the time," Officer Van Dyke replied.

"Go ahead and look for what you can. We'll do the same on our end and compare notes." The guy with all the stripes then turned to his guys. "Let's get back and shoot this up the chain. Colonel Vega is not going to be happy. Lopez, stay here and help the JS guys."

The Air Force guys, except Lopez, a guy with three stripes coming out of a star on his arm patch, went back into the tunnel. Officer Van Dyke then lifted his radio mic to his mouth.

"Dispatch, this is Van Dyke. Over."

"Dispatch here. Over," came the reply.

"Dispatch, could you contact the Dents and the Tanners, and let them know we've found Whiz and Joey. They are safe and unhurt. We'll drive them home as soon as we sort a few things out. Over."

"Should I give them an ETA? Over."

"This is complicated. Just say soon. Out."

"Ten-four, Officer Van Dyke. Out."

Officer Van Dyke turned his attention to us.

"I'm sure this is going to be quite interesting, so let's start at the top," he said.

"But, how did you know we were here?" I asked.

"In a minute, first ... what can you tell us about what happened?" asked Officer Van Dyke.

"For starters, sir," began Whiz. "They are driving a pickup truck with a heavy safe in the back and pulling a trailer with a DeLorean on it."

"A DeLorean?" asked Sergeant Lopez.

"That's what started all this," I added.

"What about the truck?" Officer Van Dyke got us back to the important stuff. "Can you describe it?"

"I was dark and far away," I replied.

"It was an older model GMC. Dark in color, maybe blue or black, but Joey is correct that we did not get a better look and cannot give a more complete description."

"But, as Whiz said, right now it's hauling a trailer with a DeLorean on it," I said.

Officer Van Dyke immediately radioed this piece of information to Jasper Springs Police Dispatch for an APB. It made me feel pretty good that something I said was important enough to be an all-points bulletin.

"Now," continued Officer Van Dyke. "Let's start at the beginning."

"But, how did you find us?" I asked, again.

"Several major clues came together, Joey. First, we received a call from your father. You were quite late for supper ... apparently well past your curfew. He called the Tanners confirming that Whiz hadn't come home either, then he called us. We radioed to our patrol cars to keep an eye out for you. Second, Lieutenant Michielini's son, Ray, heard you guys talking about exploring a hole in Mr. Zimmer's barn, and he mentioned it to his father. When all the pieces came together, I headed out here thinking maybe you got trapped somehow."

"Trapped, we were," echoed Whiz.

"But, there was more to it. We also had a call from the Air Force about an alarm going off at their installation next door. They were heading out to investigate but wanted us standing by. We do that during drills but this was the first real alarm they've had. We had no idea how you two could be caught up in an alarm at the Air Force Installation, but, Chief Reid was not happy. We sent two cars right over.

"The clincher came when Chief Master Sergeant Washington radioed over asking if I knew a Mr. Whiz Tanner or a Mr. Joey Dent."

"We found the notes you left with a description of the crime you witnessed," said Sergeant Lopez. "Our command is pretty upset. That safe contains some very valuable electronic equipment. Not to mention a year's worth of classified data we acquired with it."

"Wow," Whiz and I said, almost together.

"But now, your story," Officer Van Dyke replied.

"It all started with the DeLorean," Whiz responded.

"The DeLorean on the trailer? I thought this was about exploring a hole?" Officer Van Dyke looked puzzled.

"Chuck Boyles saw a DeLorean being pushed into Farmer Zimmer's barn here, and we came to check it out," I said.

"Joey is correct, sir," Whiz continued. "We did verify a DeLorean was in this barn yesterday morning.

We obtained several photographs to prove it to Thorny Rose and the other kids at school."

"I've always wanted to see a DeLorean." Officer Van Dyke looked around as if the car might still be there.

Sergeant Lopez nodded in agreement and also gave a quick look around.

"It looked just like that one in the *Back to the Future* movies, without that flux stuff," I said.

"If I may get back to the pertinent details," broke in Whiz. "While examining the photograph, we saw evidence of a suspicious hole along with apparently newly installed electric wiring ... and not a very professional looking installation."

"So, we came back to check it out," I added.

"Yes," broke in Whiz, again. "We used this as a training exercise while also satisfying our curiosity. When we arrived, we found Donald and Cal hauling cement chunks out of the hole. They left, and we decided to take a quick look to see what they were digging. Needless to say, we became trapped."

Between the two of us we continued the whole story, with Officer Van Dyke and Sergeant Lopez both taking notes. The Chief Master Sergeant returned and got in his own set of questions.

"Your crime report, as you titled it, says you took photographs of the intruders," the Chief Master Sergeant said.

It was a statement that was really a question.

"Yes, sir," replied Whiz, as he dug out his camera. "As they were trying to climb into your storeroom, I photographed their attempt."

He handed the camera to the Chief Master Sergeant who turned it on and scanned through the shots.

"Very well done, son," he said. "Sorry, but I'm going to take possession of this until we can copy the photos. Our investigators will want them."

"Chief," asked Officer Van Dyke. "Could you see that the Jasper Springs Police also get copies?"

"Sure thing, Officer," the Chief Master Sergeant replied.

After what seemed like an hour, everybody had asked everything they thought Whiz and I could reveal, so we were free to go.

As we were following Patrolman Edwards out to the car, Farmer Zimmer came into the barn. A whole new set of questions were beginning, but Patrolman Edwards herded us toward the car so we could not hear them. I must say, though, Farmer Zimmer did not look or sound happy—especially after seeing the piles of dirt in his barn.

CHAPTER 14
Tanner-Dent Interviewed

Patrolman Edwards opened the door at the back of the patrol car opposite from the four bulls who had all walked over to check out the late-night disturbance. Whiz and I walked from the barn to the car with our eyes on the bulls the whole time. Once in, Patrolman Edwards closed the door and signaled to the patrolman behind the wheel to go.

We drove slowly to the gate with the bulls following us. One of Farmer Zimmer's hired hands guided the bulls away, as we exited the pasture. He closed the gate, and the patrol car turned left on Jamestown Road. It was then that I realized how tired I was and how late it had become. And … our bikes were the other way. Whiz made this same observation.

"Officer?" Whiz called over the back seat. "We left our bikes in the ditch at the other end of the pasture."

The cop stopped and turned around to look at us. He didn't say anything but seemed to think about what to do. Finally, he put the car in reverse and backed up to the end of the pasture.

"Right here," I said, as we passed the spot where we hid them.

He stopped and got out. I tried to get out but the back door wouldn't open from the inside—I guess that's to keep bad guys from escaping. The officer opened my door, and both me and Whiz climbed out.

"You know you guys look ridiculous," he said, and my face felt even more itchy. "Grab your bikes, and we'll see if they fit in the trunk."

"Our Surveillance Kits are in the pasture, sir," said Whiz, and he took off over the fence before the cop, with a very puzzled look on his face, could say anything.

I grabbed my bike and brought it to the car. As the patrolman picked it up, I went back for Whiz's. We got the second bike partially into the trunk, as Whiz came out of the woods with both Surveillance Kits over one shoulder. We all climbed back into the police cruiser and headed to Jasper Springs. In addition to tiredness and lateness, I also noticed how cold it had gotten, so I got my jacket from my Surveillance Kit and put it on.

We dropped Whiz off first, since his house was closer. His parents were at the front door when we drove up—and did not look happy. His dad came over and lifted Whiz's bike out of the trunk. The two of them walked slowly to the house.

I dreaded getting to my house, but before long, we turned into my driveway. My parents were also waiting at the front door. I got out of the car. My dad, too, came to get my bike.

It was a long walk to the front door where Mom was standing. I couldn't tell which she was more of— mad or relieved. She did kiss the top of my head, as I passed through the doorway—that must count for something. When Dad came in, the mood was just as icy.

Due to the late hour, and the fact that I had school in the morning—what was I saying? It was already morning, and school was in just a few hours! A half a night's sleep wasn't going to do it for me.

Anyway, Dad said, "We'll talk about this after school. Wash that ridiculous paint off your face, get something to eat, and get to bed."

Mom brought out the supper she had been saving for me and I ate like I've never done before. Dad headed up to bed while Mom waited for me to finish eating. She mentioned a few times how worried they were, but that was the extent of any yelling I got. I listened but kept eating—I was so hungry. I ate quickly and headed up to bed—I was so tired.

When I finally lay down after an extremely long and scary day, my eyes closed instantly, and I was in dreamland. I was in a tunnel running from two giant safes. They were bearing down on me, their dials spinning, as I climbed a long ladder up to a hole in the government's atomic missile launch center. I kept running through doors as alarms went off. Before long, security guards were chasing me and screaming "halt or we'll shoot ... you trespasser!"

Just as they were closing in, and the safes were about to pounce, the alarms got louder and louder. However, the clanging bells and sirens changed into the buzz of my alarm clock, a noise I was very familiar with. I woke up. It was way too early for that—something must be wrong. But, the sun was up and shining through my window, so my clock must have been right. I got out of bed, dressed, and went downstairs.

Breakfast went without a hitch—no talk of last night's adventure, except Dad said we would have a discussion after he got home from work. I left for school—for once hoping classes would never end.

As usual, I met Whiz by the bike racks. Ray Michielini was also walking up as I arrived.

"Hey, so what happened last night? My dad said you guys broke up a secret spy ring or something."

"Not a ring," replied Whiz. "There were two guys. Joey and I—" He was about to go on, but the first bell rang—ten minutes to class.

Ray looked at his watch. "That sounds exciting, but I need to rush to get over to the high school. I'll see you guys later." He took off at a run.

On the way to the building, Whiz and I compared notes about the night before. He got a similar treatment when he got home, but his parents mentioned the word 'grounded' a few times. I guess that's the least we could expect. But we did nothing wrong. We were just exploring a tunnel in Farmer Zimmer's barn. What's so wrong with that—we shouldn't be grounded for that, right? It wasn't our fault we accidentally stumbled into a top-secret robbery!

We trudged off to class.

Just before lunch, things got exciting again. Whiz and I were both called to report to Principal

Niedermeyer's office. Uh oh. That couldn't be good. But, we weren't on school grounds, and it wasn't during school hours. What could the Principal want with us? We slunk into the main office and took a seat in the waiting area.

We didn't have to wait long before Principal Niedermeyer emerged from his office—and guess who was following him? Two Air Force officers. One had a nametag that said Vega—he must be Colonel Vega who the Chief Master Sergeant said was so upset. The second guy had two big shiny stars on his shoulders. That must mean something. They all walked over to Whiz and me. Principal Niedermeyer introduced us.

"Good morning, Joey. I'm Colonel Vega." He stuck out his hand to shake mine.

"Good morning," I mumbled back timidly.

"Good morning, Whiz," he repeated, as he got closer to Whiz.

They shook hands, too, and Whiz replied with a "good morning" quite a bit more forceful than mine.

"I'd like to introduce you to Major General Fitzgrant."

"Hello, boys. I hear we owe you a debt of gratitude for last night's …" and there was a very short pause as he seemed to pick his words carefully. "Let's just call it … an event."

He shook our hands, too, as we both said hello.

Principal Niedermeyer pointed to the conference room and we all walked into a big room with a window instead of a wall. There was a giant table in the center with fancy chairs all around it. I had seen this room many times through the big window, but I'd never been in it.

We circled around the big table, and Principal Neidermeyer sat in the biggest chair at the end, and the two Air Force guys sat on one side. Whiz and I sat opposite the Air Force after the General pointed and said, "Have a seat, boys."

The Principal started things off. "Gentlemen, I know you've gotten their parent's permission, so I hope you don't mind, but it's school board policy that a school employee remains in the room anytime outside authorities or individuals are interacting with the students."

"No problem," replied Major General Fitzgrant. "We're just going to ask standard investigation questions. We appreciate you allowing us to do so today. The sooner we get all the facts, the better the investigation will go."

Colonel Vega took over then. "Whiz and Joey, General Fitzgrant has read the reports from last night, but I'd like for you to tell him, in your own words, what happened."

We both sat there not saying anything … yet. I knew I was wondering what was going to happen if we admit to the US Air Force that we were trespassing on US Government property and that we entered a highly-classified area. I didn't know what Whiz was thinking, but the General must have read my thoughts.

"Boys," he said in a very fatherly tone. A nice one, not like the one I got last night from Dad. "The last thing we want is to waste time pursuing two young boys for accidentally becoming trapped on Air Force property. I fully understand that your presence on our side of the fence was completely accidental, and given who was chasing you, completely understandable. Now

... what can you tell me about last night, especially something that I may not have read in the report?"

That seemed to do the trick. Whiz started talking, from the beginning. "Sir, Thorny Rose and Chuck Boyles, two of our classmates from here at Jasper Springs Elementary School, were having a disagreement about the sighting of an antique DeLorean automobile ..." He kept on like this for about twenty minutes.

He mentioned the Tanner-Dent Detective Agency at least four times. When he came up for a breath, the General started asking questions.

We spent nearly an hour in that conference room. Principal Neidermeyer called for someone to bring some coffee for the adults and lemonade for me and Whiz. Both Major General Fitzgrant and Colonel Vega asked many questions. They also filled us in on some of what they had done so far. Which didn't seem to be much.

Without a license plate number, it was going to be hard to identify the truck. They were hoping that the search for a DeLorean on a trailer would be more fruitful, but they struck out there too. They were working with the Jasper Springs Police, the State Police, and even the FBI.

Nobody found any identifiable fingerprints, but they were still examining things in both the barn and the building at the other end of the tunnel. They did find some very small fingerprints, and Colonel Vega said he thought those would turn out to be mine and Whiz's.

"We have been able to recover quite a bit of evidence—DNA from blood left behind by scraped hands, tire marks in the dirt, things like that. But, the trouble is, we need a person or truck to compare those to. We haven't been able to identify the two men you saw. Having only their first names has not been very enlightening—we need something more to go on," said Major General Fitzgrant. "Apparently the name given to Mr. Zimmer when they rented the barn was a false one."

"The FBI checked with the state Department of Motor Vehicles to try to locate DeLorean owners, but they didn't find a name match," added Colonel Vega. "We're checking all the owners anyway as well as in surrounding states. But, since Cal, as you say, built his car from parts, there may not be a state registration for it. The FBI, however, is checking out purchases of DeLorean parts as well as the source of the air compressor, tools, and ladders left behind. I have great faith they will turn up something, but it's a slow process."

"We understand well the tediousness of detective work, sir," Whiz interjected.

"I'm sure you do." Colonel Vega chuckled.

Major General Fitzgrant also let out a small laugh and then became serious again.

"We'd like for you two to work with an FBI artist on putting together a likeness of Donald and Cal," said Major General Fitzgrant. "The photographs you took were a good start, but only one of the perpetrators was looking up and his face was partially obscured by his hand."

"It would be our honor," replied Whiz. "To help in any further manner we can."

"Good," said Colonel Vega. "We've arranged for an FBI artist to be at the Jasper Springs Police station this afternoon."

"We'll be there," I answered. "Unless we're grounded. Our parents weren't too happy about us being out so late."

Both Air Force officers chuckled.

"Here's my card," Colonel Vega said, as he handed business cards to both me and Whiz and one to Principal Neidermeyer. "I can't keep you from being grounded, but call if you have any other problems ... or have your parents call. And, if you can think of anything else that might be useful, give me a ring."

Not to be outdone, Whiz whipped out business cards of his own and handed one each to Major General Fitzgrant and Colonel Vega.

ⓉANNER-DENT DETECTIVE AGENCY

"We solve crimes, mysteries, problems ... "

Wilson "Whiz" Tanner
Chief Investigator

www.TannerDent.com

Both Air Force officers looked at the cards as smiles grew on their faces. Whiz then handed a third one to Principal Neidermeyer, who had more of a puzzled look.

"I knew that you two had a little game of detectives going on. I read in the *Jasper Springs News* about you, and of course, rumors around school. But, this makes it look a little more serious than that," he said.

"Rest assured, sir," answered Whiz. "The Jasper Springs Elementary School, and all of Jasper Springs, in fact, is much safer, due to the work of Tanner-Dent."

Colonel Vega tapped Whiz's card and placed it in his shirt pocket with a nod to us. Major General Fitzgrant did likewise and Principal Neidermeyer just looked concerned.

We all said goodbye and Whiz and I headed to the last few minutes of lunch period. We ate quickly and sat through the rest of the school day. It was a blur— partly because I was thinking about Air Force secrets and partly because I was still tired as a dog. I didn't know where that expression came from, but Dad said it a lot after he came home from work. I actually dozed off a few times before the final bell rang.

CHAPTER 15
The Breakthrough

After school, Whiz and I went straight to the Jasper Springs Police Headquarters to meet with the FBI artist. It took about fifteen minutes for each of us to describe Donald and Cal. The artist then went off by himself with the four drawings. About twenty minutes later, he came back with two drawings. He showed them to us separately, first to me and then to Whiz. He didn't want us to influence the other as we said what we thought.

They looked pretty good. He combined things both Whiz and I told him and they formed two quite accurate portraits. He faxed the two pictures to Colonel Vega and then left.

The rest of Monday was just as much a blur as school. After the excitement of the FBI guy, the tiredness came back stronger than ever. We both went home. I did some homework—I think—and went to bed early. I looked so tired and pitiful when Dad got home that he didn't even give me a big lecture. He just said not to enter old barns again and let it drop after I explained everything that went on.

On Tuesday, I was much more alert. Whiz told me about his encounter with his parents, and it went pretty much the same as mine. They didn't mention the word 'grounded' again, but he said his dad and mom both went on about how concerned they were at us not coming home. Like me, he promised not to do it again and they let it drop. Sometimes parents can be reasonable.

The school day was normal and I met Whiz in the Crime Lab after stopping by home to drop off my books and get a snack. He was as busy as ever when I entered.

"Agent K." He jumped right in. "I have several leads to work through, so we have a busy evening ahead of us."

"What kind of leads?" I had to ask. "There's no way we can find those guys. If the US Air Force and the FBI can't find them, what chance do we have—they have spy planes and satellites!"

"We have the advantage of seeing the perpetrators and their truck, even if our look was not superb. We also have seen the DeLorean, which lies at the heart of the leads on which I am working."

"Okay, what leads would those be, Whiz?" He gave me a stern look but didn't say anything. "Sorry, Agent M. This code name stuff seems unnecessary sometimes."

"We must establish and maintain our professionalism while in the Crime Lab, Joey." He slowly and carefully said my name. "Talking in secret will become second nature before long."

"Yeah, I got it," I replied. "So, what leads are we working on, Agent M?"

"I have been searching the Internet for DeLoreans. Here is a list of sites I want you to explore." He handed me a printout that was full of Internet addresses—URLs he called them. "While I use the Crime Computer to continue my search, you can start on these with your computer at home."

"If you've already checked these out, what am I supposed to do?"

"I only found URLs associated with DeLoreans within a 400-mile radius of Jasper Springs. We need to further examine the sites to see if we can find our DeLorean. E-mail me if you find something promising."

With my marching orders in hand, I exited the Crime Lab. The cameras showed no intruders—what did Whiz call them? Interlopers? There were no interlopers, so I left quickly, jumped on my bike, and headed for home.

At home, I settled down to some good old Internet searching. There were very few pictures, and most of the websites just pointed back to the same two or three want ads with a DeLorean for sale. The original site, from the state capital, had a comment saying the owner sold it months ago. So much for current information online.

This was becoming very boring. Detective work can be like that sometimes. Anyway, I was ready to give up for the night when I decided to try one last URL.

This one brought me to an advertisement for a car show this weekend in Jamestown, on the other side of the county. What really caught my eye, right in the middle of the screen, was a shiny DeLorean—sitting on a trailer!

Rather than sending an e-mail, I ran downstairs for the phone.

"Whiz! I found it!"

"Are you reporting Agency business on an unsecure line, Agent K?"

"Huh?"

I could hear a noisy exhale of breath over the phone line.

"What did you find, Agent K?"

He said Agent K very quietly, but I could tell he was putting a lot of emphasis on it.

"Uh, I think I found the car, Agent M. It's on the trailer and everything." I gave him the address.

"I will check it out, also. If it indeed appears to be the automobile we are seeking, I will relay the information to Officer Van Dyke. Thank you, for a job well done." We ended the call, and I headed up to bed.

<<<>>>

On Wednesday I met Whiz at the bike racks.

"No luck with Officer Van Dyke," Whiz said, as I rode up.

"He wouldn't listen?" That surprised me, since he was our one good friend on the police force.

"No, not that. He is out of town and will be until sometime next week."

"But the car show is this weekend. If they don't catch the guys by then, they'll be gone."

"I am aware of our time-imposed problem. We need to find another conduit into the police department. Patrolman Edwards would listen to us but it would be taken more seriously by the Chief if it came from someone higher up in the force. He usually listens to Officer Van Dyke."

"How about Ray's dad? If we give our clues to Ray, he could convince his dad that they should investigate. Lieutenant Michielini is almost as important as Chief Reid."

Whiz actually got a little smile on his face. "Ray would be perfect. As soon as school is out, we need to find him."

That day, school went as slowly as ever. It was getting close to the end of the grading period, so the teachers were trying to cram that last bit of knowledge into our brains before the tests on Friday. Whiz loved this part—it moved more at his pace. But, the ending bell finally rang, and we all headed out.

I met Whiz in the hall as he left the counseling center. After a quick "hey," I turned toward the front door, but Whiz gabbed my arm.

"This way, Joey," he said, as he motioned down the hallway toward the back exit. "We must head toward the high school. They still have half an hour before their final bell. That will give us time to reconnoiter and hopefully spot Ray before he leaves the school grounds."

"Reconnoiter?" I had to ask. "What does that mean?"

"The verb form of reconnaissance," he replied.
"Whiz!"
"We are going to case the joint, Joey."

"Oh, a Whiz Word for recon … like soldiers do."

Whiz just smiled. A small smile, but I could see the upturned corners of his lips.

So, we headed out the back door and crossed the football field which separates the high school from the elementary and middle schools. As we exited the field, we quickly spotted all the doors on the near side of the high school. If Ray was heading straight home, he would probably come out of one of those.

"We shall set up our surveillance in front of the second door," Whiz said as he pointed toward the nearest door to our left. "We can still watch the other doors, but this one is closer to more classrooms, so it is likely he will exit through it."

"What if his locker is closer to one of the other doors?"

This seemed to startle Whiz a bit. We didn't have lockers so he probably didn't think of that. But last year my sister, Patty, graduated from Jasper Springs High, and for years I heard all about her locker—so, I knew about lockers.

"Agent K," he responded. "That possibility did not cross my mind. Given that new angle, I suppose if we hang out right here, we can watch all four doors and still see the sidewalk in front. No matter where he exits, he must pass within our eyesight … if he is heading home."

We climbed onto the block wall at the edge of the parking lot, sat, and waited. Before long, high-schoolers came pouring out of the building. Whiz took the front two doors and the sidewalk running in front of the school. I took the back two doors. The kids started filling the walkways, some heading toward the bike racks, some toward cars, and some out to the street. It was hard to single out the faces in such a crowd, but we were trained detectives—we could handle it.

As the high school kids flowed past, we got a few strange looks. I was starting to think this wouldn't work, when Whiz hit my arm.

"Over there." He pointed. "I see Ray in front of the school."

I looked where he was pointing. Ray was on the front sidewalk, walking along Moulton Street with a couple of other guys.

"Hurry or we won't catch him," I said, as we both dropped to the ground.

We started running. Ray wasn't running but he did have quite a head start and was walking at a good clip. We kept moving and caught him before he reached Broad Way.

He and his friends were very animated, waving their arms as they pointed at the sky a lot.

"Ray!" I yelled.

He stopped.

"Ray Michielini," Whiz yelled a bit louder.

Ray turned around to see us storming down on him like a SWAT team.

"Hey, guys. What's up?"

"We are in need of your assistance," Whiz blurted out.

Ray turned to his buddies. "I'll catch up to you later."

"Don't get too caught up playing with the little kids … we've got flying to talk about," one of them said, making a swirling motion with his hands, as he chuckle in our direction. "Tomorrow, we drone!"

"Yeah, tomorrow," Ray replied. Then he turned to us. "Okay ... so, you need some spying done at the big school."

"Actually," I cut in, wondering what they were going to drone about, but I pushed that thought out of my mind. "We need your dad's help, but we need you to ask for it."

"We think we found the DeLorean that this top-secret Air Force case hinges upon," said Whiz.

"Just call the police. You don't need my dad."

"Officer Van Dyke is out of town and the Chief never listens to us," I said.

"Precisely," interjected Whiz. "If you could convince your father that we have a possible lead, he may be able to get Chief Reid to check it out. It may be our only hope."

"Well, how do I know you have a good lead?" replied Ray. "If I'm going out on a limb for you guys, I need to be convinced first."

"Fair enough," offered Whiz. He then looked at me. "Joey, time is of the essence."

"Okay," I said. "So?"

"I think we need to break protocol and bring Ray to the Crime Lab."

Whoa! That is a big break in Agency procedures, whatever protocol meant. "Are you sure?" I asked.

"As I said ... time is of the essence." He turned to Ray. "Can you keep a secret?"

"A top secret?" Ray asked with a big grin.

"Bigger." Whiz gave him a very serious look.

"Your crime lab? I gotta see this. So, sure, I can keep a secret," Ray replied—still with the grin.

"We need to go to my house."

We started running.

"Hold on, speedy," Ray called out. "I'm not running after a couple of elementary kids all the way to your house. I'll meet you there."

Since there was no need for us to get there before Ray, Whiz and I returned to our school to get our bikes. We caught up with Ray before he made it to Whiz's and matched his pace.

When we arrived at Whiz's driveway, Whiz skidded to a halt in front of Ray—blocking his movement. Maybe he thought better of it and was going to back out of letting Ray see the Crime Lab. But, that's not what happened.

"Ray?" Whiz said.

"What now?" came the reply.

"What Joey and I are about to show you is very secret. We are counting on you not telling anyone what you are about to see."

"I got it. I said I can keep a secret."

"This way," said Agent M.

CHAPTER 16
From Breakthrough to Bust to Drone

We both followed Whiz to the back of the garden shed, where he bent down and pressed the fake knot. I was watching Ray. His face had a strange look when the hidden speaker asked, "name?" and it kept getting stranger as Whiz went through the entire ritual.

When the door panel popped open, I grabbed it and opened it all the way. Whiz entered and Ray slowly stepped in—not sure what he was getting into. Whiz was already climbing down the stairs as I entered and shut the door, triggering the black light. The white surgical tape on the edge of the steps glowed as Ray and I descended.

At the bottom, Whiz opened the last door and everybody walked into the Headquarters of the Tanner-Dent Detective Agency—our Crime Lab.

"Wow," Ray said, as he looked around. "This is amazing."

"At Tanner-Dent, we pride ourselves on maintaining a state-of-the-art lab for analyzing any clues we may find on a case," replied Whiz.

"Most police departments are envious of what we've built," I gushed.

"But, now … to work," said Whiz, as he walked over to the Crime Computer.

He clicked a few keys to bring up the photos he had downloaded earlier. Ray looked around the Lab as he made his way over to Whiz. He stood behind, looking over his shoulder.

"Yeah, those look like DeLoreans," Ray said.

"You'll notice that one." I pointed. "Is on a trailer. While we can't prove it's the same trailer, you've got to admit that having two DeLoreans in the county that need to be hauled on a trailer would be some coincidence. And, as we say in the Agency, there're no coincidences in detective work."

"Okay," said Ray. "Print this along with a couple of the DeLorean in Farmer Zimmer's barn. I'll take them home and see what my dad has to say."

"Could you please give us a call when your father makes a decision?" asked Whiz, as he handed Ray a business card.

Ray took the card and gave another little laugh. "You guys are playing this detective stuff to the hilt, aren't you?"

"Rest assured," Whiz responded. "This is not play."

Ray put up his hands. "No offense intended, Whiz. I kinda admire it."

Ray picked up the pictures as they spit out of the printer and left. Less than an hour later, he called to say his dad was on board. He would fill in Chief Reid tonight. If the Chief agreed, he would call the Jamestown police and they would check it out, since it was out of the Jasper Springs jurisdiction.

With nothing pressing to do, this was a perfect opportunity to head over to the Public Works field and join whatever pick-up game was going on. But, as I left the Crime Lab, it began to rain—so I headed home to finish up some homework. End of period tests were around the corner, after all.

<<<>>>

On Thursday morning, Whiz and I parked our bikes in the school bike racks and ran down to the corner to wait for Ray as he walked by on his way to the high school. We desperately wanted to find out what Chief Reid could dig up. But, there was no sign of him by the time the warning bell rang, so we ran off to class. It was a long day.

Finally, the last bell of the day rang and I bolted out of Mrs. Truman's classroom to meet up with Whiz. We both ran, nearly full speed, through the hallway and out the back door. We made it through the football field in record time and took up our surveillance post at the front of the school this time.

Before long, the high-schoolers came rushing out of the building and onto the sidewalk. We stayed out of the way as we watched for Ray. I must say, just like before, we got some unfriendly looks from the big kids. I guess they didn't like us trespassing on their turf. But, we didn't give in. We stayed where we could watch the front door, and we waited. And waited. And waited.

The crowd trickled down to just a kid or two every now and then and pretty soon, several minutes would go by with nobody exiting. Then ten minutes passed. No Ray, and we were getting bored.

"I suppose we missed him somehow, Joey," said Whiz.

"Well, I'm heading home, then."

We walked rather fast down the street toward the elementary school bike racks, retrieved our bikes, and rode off.

"Meet me in the Crime Lab, later," Whiz called, as he turned into his driveway.

I replied, "Will do," as I kept going straight. At home, I dropped off my bookbag and got myself a snack. Nobody else was around, so I wrote Mom a note and headed back to Whiz's.

Whiz had his head buried in the Crime Computer monitor as I entered the Lab.

"What's up?" I asked.

"Still researching DeLoreans. We must stay ahead of the game in case our first lead does not pan out."

Whiz then pulled his head back and looked quizzically at the screen.

"Okay, now what's up?" I asked.

"Ray."

I came around the desk and looked over Whiz's shoulder. He clicked the mouse and brought the two small pictures from the corner of the monitor to full screen. We saw Ray on the spy cameras. He ran from the driveway to the back of the shed and began pounding on the secret door.

"We better let him in before he draws too much attention to himself," said Whiz, as he pressed the button that released the latch.

As I opened the bottom door, Ray closed the top one. The black light came on, but the light from inside the Crime Lab gave him plenty of light to see. Ray rushed down, several steps at a time.

"The Chief is really mad at you guys ... and me, too," said Ray, gasping heavily, as he tried to catch his breath.

"You mean it wasn't our DeLorean?" I asked.

"Right, but my dad says not to worry. False alarms happen all the time. They're used to it. Police are always chasing down tips that lead nowhere."

"They are quite sure about the veracity of the DeLorean at the car show?" asked Whiz, in his strange way.

"Definitely," Ray answered. "It belongs to a collector who travels around to car shows all over the country. In fact, last weekend, when your DeLorean was in Farmer Zimmer's barn, with a broken engine, the mayor of St. Louis was driving this car around a track, as a pace car for a charity race, in Missouri."

"We knew it was a long shot," added Whiz. "However, we all thought it was worth checking out."

"I know," Ray continued. "Also ... Chief Reid instructed me to tell you to stay out of police business. He really said a lot more, but it all boiled down to that. Like I said, he's mad."

"We are only doing simple, and legal, Internet searches. It just so happens that we found a very compelling clue that showed potential to lead somewhere significant," offered Whiz.

"Well, I would stay out of Chief Reid's way if I were you. My dad said the Chief was fuming after Chief Shaddock, from Jamestown, phoned him that it was a dead-end."

"The Chief never has liked us," I put in.

"Be that as it may," broke in Whiz. "We are also at a dead-end."

"Well, if you find anything thing else, I'd be interested in hearing it. But, I doubt I could be of any more help with the police."

After a few minutes of discussing possible next moves—all of which seemed to lead nowhere—Ray looked at his watch. "Hey, guys, this is interesting, and all, but it's after four o'clock, and soon I'm going to take possession of a fantastic new drone."

"Wow," I said. "I've never seen a drone before ... except on TV."

"A buddy of mine has an uncle who owns the Radio Shack out at the county mall and he's getting three of us a great deal. We're meeting him at the Public Works field in about fifteen minutes. You guys are welcome to come watch us fly."

"You bet!" I nearly yelled.

I looked at Whiz and he definitely looked interested, but he kept looking back at the Crime Computer. Then, he made a decision.

"We might as well join you," responded Whiz. "I was going to make another attempt at an Internet search, but this may be a closed case for us. I can do it later."

I didn't see Whiz giving up very often on a search for clues, but, a drone is pretty cool—even for Whiz. Maybe, especially for Whiz.

"Okay!" I agreed, as I put my coat on.

Whiz and I rode our bikes slowly beside Ray as he walked. The Public Works building was only a couple of blocks away, so it didn't take long to get there. Another excited high-schooler was already waiting as we arrived.

The wait wasn't long. Soon a car pulled up in the parking lot and Ray and the other kid ran over to it. The driver got out, holding a box and whooping it up. He handed the box to Ray and reached inside his car for an identical box, which he handed to the other kid. Then, he ducked back in for one more box, and the three of them dashed out onto the open field.

Almost as one, they opened the boxes and pulled out the three identical drones. They spent a few minutes attaching things and were ready to fly.

"I don't know how much charge you guys have," said the driver. "I was charging my battery on the drive from the mall."

"We'll fly 'til it dies!" yelled Ray.

"Ditto!" yelled the second guy.

Ray placed his on top of the box to keep the rotor blades from chewing up grass as it took off. After playing around with the controls to make sure everything was working properly, he moved one of the levers all the way. Whiz and I both looked up as it flew straight up. The other two drones quickly joined it. It looked cool.

"This would be great for our detective work," said Whiz, as he kept his eyes on the flying machines.

"Just wait until we get cameras!" yelled Ray to the other two. "We'll have the coolest spy drones in town."

Whiz turned to look at me, but he had that faraway gaze that means his brain is in overdrive. "We have cameras," he said.

The three high-schoolers each glanced over at Whiz.

"You don't mean our lookout cameras, do you?" I inquired. "We need those for security."

Whiz ignored my comment.

"Our security cameras are quite small and lightweight. They should be perfect for your drones."

"Having a drone with a camera would be super cool," said Ray. "Would you let us use them?"

"Perhaps we can work a deal," replied Whiz. I could almost see the brain gears whirling.

Ray and the others smiled but turned their attention back to the drones. I pulled Whiz aside.

"But, Whiz ... we need those cameras for headquarters security."

"I admit, they do add a needed level of security to the Crime Lab. However, there are problems with them. For instance, they must be constantly recharged. I have had to do so several times since we installed them. We must work on a better method ... possibly running wires to them. In the meantime, we have a bargaining chip for testing out a drone for future surveillance work."

The guys flew for several minutes, making big circles that got farther and farther away. Ray had flown his over the Public Works building toward Jefferson Boulevard and back. His was running low on battery and began to descend. He landed it in the middle of the field.

"Well, that's it for me," said Ray. "Home for a full recharge."

As he was running back from retrieving his drone, the second one did the same thing. The last one kept going.

Ray and the second guy put their drones back in the boxes.

"See you guys right here tomorrow after school," called the third guy.

"You got it," said Ray.

Four of us started walking, leaving the last guy flying his drone. At the road, Whiz and I turned left while the others turned right—Ray stopped.

"So, guys," he called to us. "Let's talk cameras."

CHAPTER 17
A Dead-End Leads to Inspiration

Friday morning came as it always does at the end of every school week, but this one was a bit depressing. The Tanner-Dent Detective Agency was on the verge of its first failure—and it was a big one.

We witnessed the stealing of a top-secret safe, right before our eyes, and were helpless to stop it. What's worse, we weren't anywhere near solving it even though we had so many clues. We even saw the culprits and knew their names—their first names anyway. Since we didn't hear anything new from Colonel Vega, we guessed they didn't catch anybody they wanted us to identify. Of course, Chief Reid wouldn't tell us anything even if he knew something.

Tanner-Dent was too new of a detective agency to have this big of a failure. It would probably destroy us, or at the very least, demote us to only solving cases involving missing lunchboxes or lost cats—which we've done our fair share of, but only while we were between real cases. As bad as I felt, I'm sure Whiz felt even worse.

I finished off breakfast and biked to school. Whiz was already there, parking his bike as I rode up.

"I uncovered no new leads," he said, as I shoved my bike into the rack. "But, I may have worked out a deal with Ray to borrow his drone tomorrow. It will cost us one of our surveillance cameras, but I feel it will be worth it to see if a drone would be a worthy expense for Tanner-Dent."

I'm not sure if my excitement at flying a drone outweighed my disappointment at being at a dead-end in our case, but, wow! I'm gonna fly a drone! Maybe.

"But what about our case?" I asked. "Certainly, there are more places we could find a DeLorean."

"I suggest we close this case and move on. We could plan for a weekend of training to give our minds something positive to work on, and if things work out with Ray, we have tomorrow free to test the drone with a camera. The Case of the Stolen Safe has effectively ended … for us. Donald and Cal are probably in a foreign land by now and I am quite sure they would have already turned the safe over to their boss."

I could see that the slim chance of flying a drone with a camera brightened Whiz's day, but the loss of a case still gave him that low-energy look he gets when things don't go right. His words showed acceptance, but his mood showed otherwise.

The first bell rang and we headed to class for another wasted day. Blah, blah, blah … I couldn't even bring myself to describe how boring and sad it was. The whole day was terrible—oh, and we had end of term tests in almost every subject. This day was so depressing. But, seeing Whiz with no energy was what really sent it downhill for me—he's usually up on test day, very up.

But, then the day turned in our favor. When we got to the bike rack after school, there was a note stuck to Whiz's handlebars.

> # Meet me at the Public Works field at 5:00. Bring a camera. Drone time! Ray

"Well," said Whiz. "It appears that we may be close to a deal with Ray."

Of course, at five o'clock on the dot, we were in the Public Works parking lot waiting for Ray. Whiz had removed one of the surveillance cameras, charged it, and brought it along.

When Ray and the other two drove up, Ray climbed out of the back seat and walked over to us.

"You bring the camera?" asked Ray.

"Do we get to fly?" responded Whiz.

Ray seemed to hesitate for just a moment, but a big smile gave away his answer. He really wanted that camera.

"You give me a camera and you can fly it for a few minutes."

"Well, Ray …" began Whiz, and then he paused.

He pulled the camera out of his coat pocket and turned it over in his hand. I've never seen Whiz negotiate before. This was interesting.

"This camera is quite valuable. But, I am convinced that you already know this or you would have purchased one with the drone."

"So, what'll it take for me to get the camera?"

"If you let Joey and me fly the drone today, we will let you use …" and he said 'use' very slowly, "The camera for the rest of the day."

"I'm not talking about borrowing, I'm talking about keeping." Ray's smile was dwindling a bit.

"If you let us use the drone this weekend for some extended surveillance testing, we may see clear to let you have the camera." Whiz stretched out his hand to offer Ray the camera. "Deal?"

Ray didn't hesitate. He grabbed the camera and turned it over examining it.

"Okay. I borrow it for today and let you two take turns flying it for a few minutes. Then, we'll discuss what it will take for me to keep the camera."

"Hey, that sounds like a deal to me," I said, with a big ol' smile forming on my face.

Ray attached the camera to his drone, synced it to his smart phone, and sent it flying.

"Wow!" everybody said, at different times, as we all watched the video sent back from Ray's drone.

The other two guys got their drones flying and they did a little dogfighting while we all watched on the phone. True to his word, Ray let me and Whiz take turns controlling the drone.

I flew it over the Public Works building and lowered it so that we couldn't see it at all. I kept flying it by looking only at the video feed on the phone. This was cool. Whiz tried the same thing but couldn't keep it as steady as I could.

I hovered it close to the window of my dad's office and got really close to the glass. I could see my dad at his desk as he was cleaning up to go home. This would be fantastic for spying on crooks. We needed one of these.

All too soon, it was time to end our fun. Whiz and I had to go home for dinner, so Ray took control back.

"Now the deal is," said Ray. "I keep the camera for the rest of the day and then we discuss what it takes for me to keep it. Right?"

"Right," agreed Whiz. "We will talk to you tomorrow."

With that, we climbed on our bikes and left. On the ride, we talked about all the things we could do with an airborne camera until it was time to split up and head to our own homes. Tomorrow was going to be interesting!

After dinner, I played some computer games and watched a little TV. To give us a rest after test day, there was no homework, so the weekend was free. I did a little web surfing about drones and then climbed into bed about a half an hour earlier than normal for a weekend night. DeLoreans and top-secret safes were the last things on my mind.

Putting my headboard nightlight on, I started reading a book—something new that Mom picked up and thought I would like—*Howard Wallace, PI.* Even though I'm a professional detective, I still like reading about fictional kid detectives. Whiz does, too. But, he reads much more than I do. I opened the book and immediately perked up.

At the beginning of the book, Howard has a list of *Rules of Private Investigation*. I read the list. This guy was pretty good. He had the start of his own TTP in this short list. Two items really caught my eye—the first one and the tenth. These got me thinking anew about our current case—or non-case, since it was over.

Howard says, in his first rule, to "work with what you've got." Well, we've got a lot of real evidence—not hearsay or third-party stuff, but real honest-to-goodness eyewitness evidence. Whiz and I actually witnessed the crime. We saw the criminals, we saw the car and the truck, we heard that they were going to give the safe to someone else who would pay them a bunch of money. We knew that Cal loved his car, but he must get rid of it so he could flee with his money, and the money is worth way more than the car.

Then I thought about the tenth rule, "pick your battles." The reputation of the Tanner-Dent Detective Agency rested on this case. If this wasn't a battle worth fighting, then we should get out of the business. Who's going to hire us to solve a crime if we couldn't solve one we were smack in the middle of? I had to report this to Headquarters. Agent M needed to know.

I got out of bed and composed an e-mail. As soon as it looked right, I zipped it off to Headquarters. Smiling, at a job well done, I headed back to bed.

Feeling much happier, I sat up in bed and read a couple of chapters of *Howard Wallace, PI.* to see what else this kid had to offer. Life was back to good and soon I was tired enough to put the book down and close my eyes—that's when life went from good to exciting.

I had turned off my headboard light, but my room didn't go completely dark all at once. There was a flash. Then another. Pulses of light were flashing through my bedroom window. On and off, like Morse code.

Whiz! He got my message. Or, he got the drone. Either way, tomorrow was looking to be a much better day.

CHAPTER 18
An Invisible Clue in a Picture

The next morning, I rushed to Whiz's house just as the secret flashing message instructed. When I entered the Crime Lab, Whiz was sitting at the Crime Computer, moving the mouse around, clicking away. Ray's drone was also sitting on the desk—our surveillance camera still attached.

"Fantastic, Agent M," I said, as I threw my coat on a chair and closed in for a good look at the drone. "I take it this is what last night's emergency signal was all about?"

"Actually no, Agent K. Your message prompted that summons. I only worked a deal with Ray this morning. He works at Johnny's Pizza on Saturdays so he is unable to fly it anyway. We get the drone until he gets off work and he gets to keep the camera."

"So, my message made you see that we shouldn't give up on the case?"

"More than that. I found the thieves, thanks to you, Agent K," Whiz replied.

"What?" I cried.

Whiz always amazed me with the stuff he does or figures out. He shouldn't surprise me anymore. But, he still does.

"How?"

"Your message got me thinking in a direction I was not originally following."

"What direction?" I asked.

I think my mouth was still hanging open, as I was staring at the drone I would be flying today.

"The most important thing is … this battle is worth a fight. We must save the good name of Tanner-Dent," he responded. "The second is, Cal's love of the DeLorean. But before we get too distracted … who is Howard? There are no Howards in Jasper Springs Elementary."

"Howard Wallace," I replied. "P.I."

Whiz just looked at me. I looked at him with a similar expression. Is it possible that I read a book that the Great Book Wizard of Jasper Springs didn't know about?

"A book. I read a book."

"Oh," he said, nodding his head. A small twinkle in his eye let me know he approved.

"It's a book my mom bought. I'll lend it to you. When I read his first rule, I thought about everything we had to work with and it's quite a lot."

"Your list and Howard's rules made me realize that the DeLorean is the major clue, around which this whole case revolves. We cannot abandon it. That car meant too much to Cal. He would not just leave it while he fled to Mexico or someplace else. He would want the car to be in the hands of someone who would appreciate it as much as he does."

"That makes sense," I said. "But who'd that be?"

"Well, working with what you have, how would you get rid of the car in a hurry?"

"I guess I would start by asking my friends if they wanted it. Then, I would advertise it on one of those websites where you can sell things."

"Precisely. But more specifically, a website that caters to the DeLorean automobile. I found such a site and I found our DeLorean on it. Therefore, I know where the automobile is ... or was on Thursday."

"Wow! Are you sure it's our car? We can't give Chief Reid another false lead."

"I am quite confident." Whiz looked at me calmly and said, "Take a look at the Crime Computer screen."

I walked behind the desk and looked. It displayed a website showing an advertisement for cars—mostly DeLoreans. Whiz clicked on one of the pictures and then he clicked the mouse a few more times and brought up the picture of the DeLorean in the barn, putting the two side by side.

"Okay, so it looks like they're both DeLoreans. But, all DeLoreans look the same ... they don't even have different paint colors since they're not even painted. I read that they're made from polished stainless steel ... no paint."

"Observe, Agent K. There is a series of scratches on the front fender of both cars. It is not so easy to see in our dark picture, but they are there."

I looked, and they both did seem to have similar scratches.

"They could be the same car, M," I responded.

"*Could be* is the key phrase. In light of our earlier false clue, we cannot take chances. We must check it out first for ourselves."

"How're we gonna do that? There's no address in the ad, and there's nothing in the picture that gives away its location. How do we know where to go? Are we gonna to call up and make an appointment?"

"We know the location."

In Whiz's typical fashion, he's saying *we* when he means *him*.

"Yeah, but the website only gives a phone number. How do you know the location?"

"Geotags," he replied.

"Agent M, you've come up with some pretty strange Whiz Words before but this is a topper. What are geotags?"

"Geotagging is the embedding of a geographic coordinate location in a file or, in our case, a photograph. It is actually an element of data containing the latitude and longitude of a point somewhere on the earth."

"Are you saying that the picture gave you the latitude and longitude of the crook's hideout?"

"Almost," he responded. "The picture showed me where the DeLorean is, and given how much he talked about that car, Cal is probably not too far away."

"You're talking in circles, M. How could you possibly know the location of the car, from a picture? I don't see any hints at where this car might be." I looked even closer to see if I missed something.

"As I said—geotags."

"I think I need a little more information. Granted you can point to a location on a map if you have the coordinates. But, where could you get those? The ground around this car doesn't show lines like on a map." I chuckled a little at that. Whiz didn't.

"I downloaded the picture file from this webpage. Digital photographs have metadata included in the file."

"Whoa, what's metadata? You're getting way off in Whiz Word World again."

"Metadata is basically a list of information about the file. In this case a picture file. It has things like dimensions, time created, type of file, and more importantly for us ... geotags. The camera, or smart phone, that took this photo has GPS capability and used the GPS satellites to determine exactly where the camera was as it took the picture. It included that information in the picture file."

"Why don't we see it on the screen?"

"Only part of the picture file contains the picture. The display program ignores the rest of the file, as if it was invisible." Whiz clicked a few more times and opened another file. "This is a program I wrote in the Python computer language ... you should learn it. It will enable you to do amazing things. Anyway, this program reads the whole picture file and, using regular expressions, pulls out the date and geotag information."

"Wow," was all I could think to say, mainly because I didn't know what regular expressions were, and I didn't want to ask because that would get Whiz sidetracked.

"This photograph was taken two days ago, and here ..." he punched in the numbers on the screen to a mapping program, "is where the car was at that time."

The mapping program showed a little balloon arrow in the backyard of a house. Whiz zoomed out, and we could see the neighborhood. The backyard where the geotag pointed was at the edge of a farm field. He zoomed out some more, and a town came into view. The house was at the edge of a small town, and another zoom-out showed the interstate just to the south.

"Hey, that looks like Woodhaven," I exclaimed.

"It certainly is," Whiz confirmed.

"Let's call Officer Van Dyke."

"Officer Van Dyke is still out of town and, given our last false alarm, no one else on the force will entertain our lead if we have no concrete evidence to back it up. No, Agent K, we must investigate further before we turn this *potential* clue over to the authorities." He really emphasized the word 'potential.' "We have to make sure the DeLorean is still there and is the right one. Also, you know what Chief Reid said … if he even thinks we are still investigating this case he will lock us up for interference."

"I guess," I replied. "But how do we investigate further? The DeLorean is in Woodhaven."

"I already checked the bus schedule. We have enough funds in our treasury to purchase two round-trip tickets, and the next bus leaves at ten o'clock. The return bus leaves Woodhaven at two p.m. We have plenty of time to get to Woodhaven, do our investigation, and get home before anyone misses us."

I swallowed hard. A bus trip to Woodhaven? We'd never done that before, not even with our parents. I guessed Whiz assumed I would agree, because he reached over and pulled our money box out of the desk drawer. Of course, he was right.

"I have taken the liberty of stocking two Surveillance Kits for our excursion. I borrowed my dad's laptop to monitor the drone's camera and I fully charged all batteries. Now, I suggest we make plans for catching that bus."

"We're taking Ray's drone?" I asked.

"I can see no better way to test the surveillance camera and determine its usefulness to our Agency than to fly over and examine the only clue we have on our biggest existing case."

I couldn't argue with that logic, but I sure hoped nothing happened to Ray's drone.

Whiz placed the laptop in his Surveillance Kit and I put the drone control in mine. The drone was too big to fit. We'd have to carry that ourselves.

I headed home to let Mom know I wouldn't be home for lunch and then I got a few bucks from my emergency money stash—just in case there was something to buy in Woodhaven.

Skipping lunch was no big deal—Whiz and I often went hiking, biking, or some other day-long excursion on Saturdays. After making a deal with Mom to finish my chores tonight, she packed a small lunch for me and I headed out. Just before ten o'clock, I met Whiz at the bike rack in the park next to the courthouse, and we waited for the bus to arrive. It came in right on time and unloaded two guys.

We quickly climbed into the bus and Whiz paid the driver for two round-trip tickets to Woodhaven. Whiz handed me my tickets, and we each stuck one into the electronic ticket machine and waited for the beep that indicated it read it. I had a big smile on my face as we walked back to our seats.

The trip took about an hour and wound through various farm fields and wooded areas. The bus didn't take County Road 18, the most direct route, but rather Jefferson Boulevard which is also State Route 68, a much bigger road with a higher speed limit.

The bus got off the main road a couple of times to stop in small towns along the way—nobody got on. We passed Indian Lake, but it looked deserted compared to when I came up here in the summer. At the interstate, we turned west for a few miles and exited at Woodhaven. The bus stopped in front of the Woodhaven Post Office and we got off. I'd never been this far from home without my parents—making it a little bit exciting while also a little bit scary.

CHAPTER 19
The Airborne Camera

Woodhaven is a very small town, a village, actually. The sign I read, as we rode in, said the population was 898. But, someone had painted a line through the last eight and wrote a seven. I guess someone left town and wanted everyone to know it. I started to walk down the street looking at things, until I noticed the street sign on the corner.

"Hey, Whiz!" I pointed at the sign. "This is Jasper Springs Road."

"It is also County Road 18, as you can see by that sign." He pointed to a road sign near the street sign. "It becomes Livermore when you reach Jasper Springs. Interestingly, Livermore was named Woodhaven Trace until the 1920s. It was quite common to name a road for the town it led to."

Some of that I knew and some I didn't, but I still thought it was a big deal that there's a Jasper Springs Road way up here in Woodhaven—even Jasper Springs doesn't have one.

"According to my measurements and Google Maps," said Whiz, as he got right down to business. "The yard we must investigate is about a half mile to the northeast."

"So, we head up Jasper Springs Road." I smiled.

"Yes," replied Whiz, showing no hint at how interesting I thought that was. "And, looking right on Decker Lane, we should see the house, on the left, three houses down."

We started walking, but I kept looking around. This was my first trip to Woodhaven and it was very different from Jasper Springs or even Belmont Village—so much smaller with no tall buildings. Across from the post office was a grocery store with gas pumps and a few other small shops that looked like someone's home with a sign on the front porch. They probably were someone's home at one time—maybe some still are.

A block away, the store signs ended, and it was obvious the rest were real houses. We kept walking until we reached Decker. This was the last street in town. Beyond it was nothing but farm fields.

"There is the object of our search, Agent K," announced Whiz—no more Joey and Whiz, we were hot on a case.

"That's not the pickup." I motioned to a truck in the driveway.

"Agreed," replied Whiz. "Too light in color."

It was only then that I thought to ask. "Whiz, uh, Agent M, are the geotags in a camera very accurate?

Perhaps they took this picture a mile from here. The reason I ask is I read that the military control the satellites that run all that GPS stuff, and they don't let civilians have access to the really good software they use."

"What you heard is correct, but even civilian equipment using those satellites are accurate to within ten or fifteen feet. So, we may not know which corner of the yard held the car, but it most assuredly was in that yard."

"Do we just walk down the street and see if we can see the DeLorean?"

"No, K. We will continue up Jasper Springs Road to the farm fields."

He gave a little pause when he said Jasper Springs Road. Maybe he thought that was cool too.

So, that's what we did. A few yards beyond the corner lot, we climbed over a ditch and entered the farm field. Being late in the season, there was nothing planted in it. I was hoping for some tall corn stalks or something to help hide us—we had nothing. There was a line of trees at the edge between the houses and the field, so that helped. We strolled along as if we were just a couple of kids out walking in the field—not two highly-trained detectives investigating stolen Air Force secrets.

Just past the corner yard, Whiz put out his hand in a silent gesture to stop. We both stopped and stooped down.

"I see the car," Whiz exclaimed.

It was not on a trailer but it was a DeLorean.

"It's too far to see any scratches from here," I replied, wondering how we were going to prove this was the same DeLorean.

"One more clue that does not show up very well in the dark photo, Agent K." Whiz pulled out a printout of the car from the barn. "Look closely at the tires."

Even with the flash making it bright enough to make out that it was a DeLorean, it was still too dark for many details, but the tires were different. The front tire in the photo appeared to have whitewalls.

"Whitewalls?" I asked. "I don't remember ever seeing a whitewall tire on a real car. In old movies, yeah, but not on an actual car."

"We must get a look at the driver's side front tire, Agent K."

I looked around the back yard for a safe way to approach the car. There was none.

"You want us to crawl up? There's no way to hide along the way."

"It may come to that, but for now, we will use technology to help gather clues. Here is where the drone pays for itself." After placing the drone gently on the ground, he pulled his dad's laptop out of his Surveillance Kit and opened it. "Get the drone controls and we shall see what this device can do."

That was a relief. I pulled out the control box and flipped the on switch.

Whiz did likewise to the camera. After a few taps on the mousepad we saw, on the laptop monitor, everything that the camera saw.

"Time to gather evidence," Whiz exclaimed, as he hit the record button on the laptop. "Test the controls to make sure everything works and I will handle the video and photographs."

"Me? Flying it?"

"It is the pragmatic thing to do. You were better at controlling it than I, and that will leave me free to concentrate on recording evidence."

"Sure thing!" I said.

So, I tested the controls. I made the rotors spin and even had it lift off the ground a few inches. Then I spun it left and right and moved it slowly forward and backward.

"All set," I reported.

"Then, check out the DeLorean. Get close to the front fender and try to point the camera at the damage and the whitewall tire."

"It's a bit hard to see the car from here."

"Quite right," said Whiz, as he looked around the yard. "You will have to fly much of the journey using only the camera. But, we still need to be more secluded. Here, we can easily be seen from Jasper Springs Road … come on!"

When Whiz is hot on the trail of something it's impossible to talk him out of it. Of course, this time was no exception. Whiz picked up the drone and laptop and pushed through the trees that lined the farm field. Like always, I followed.

We ducked down behind a bunch of rusty yard equipment stacked in the corner of the lot. Whiz was already looking over at the house. I was looking everywhere else to make sure no one was watching us— if I didn't cover Whiz's back, who would? I had to admit, though, this spot was more hidden from view than the farm field.

"I perceive no movement around the house, K," Whiz whispered. "Time to proceed."

He set the drone down and I slowly pushed on the lever. The drone lifted off about twenty feet in the air. I watched it as Whiz watched the laptop monitor.

"Okay,   toward   the   automobile," he commanded.

I spun the drone so the camera faced forward and then guided it over to the car. As I lowered it, I had to switch to the camera to see where the drone was heading. The computer monitor showed a full screen view of whatever I pointed the drone toward. I made a sweep of the house, concentrating on the doors, as the drone slipped behind the car. With a slow twisting of the controls, I pointed the camera first at the scratches and then a bit lower to see the tire.

"Whitewall!" I exclaimed.

"Shhh!" replied Whiz as he repeatedly hit a key that saved screen captures. When he nodded his head, signaling that we got the pictures we needed, I pushed the lift lever all the way to climb about fifty feet as fast as I could. Then I guided it back to us and lowered it.

"This has to be our DeLorean, Whiz, uh, Agent M. We should call the Woodhaven police."

"This is our car to be sure, K. But, we do not know for certain that Donald and Cal are here. They may have sold the car and left the country. Also, Woodhaven does not have a police department. They rely on the county sheriff—I checked."

"Then what do we do?"

"We need to find out if our culprits are here. If so, we can call the Jasper Springs Police and relay that vital information. They should know whom to call. Or …" and he paused for a moment. "We can call the Air Force directly. In either case, we need to get a closer look … inside the house."

"What?" I nearly yelled.

"Relax, Agent K," said Whiz. "We have a drone, remember?"

"Oh, I thought you wanted to crawl up to the house to look in."

"Let technology do the dangerous part, Agent K. That is precisely why we have it."

"What if they see the drone? We could be arrested as Peeping Toms."

"That is a minor concern, Agent K. Our top priority is to ascertain the whereabouts of Donald and Cal. If they are in the house, we can set our trap in motion."

"We have a trap?"

"That is step two. First, we need to accomplish step one."

"Okay. But, what's ascertain?"

"Determine, learn, discover. We need to find out if they are inside."

I thumbed back on the control lever and the drone lifted off, again. Whiz started the recording. Once again, I flew the drone about twenty feet up and turned it toward the house. Using the camera feed on the laptop, I was able to maneuver the drone out to Decker Lane. I wanted to keep some distance between the drone and the house as I pointed the camera at each window, trying to find one we could see into.

Eventually, I worked the drone completely around the house but it was obvious that we could not see in from that distance.

"Agent K, proceed to the big picture window at the front and fly as close as you can get. That window will be our best chance of seeing inside."

I pointed the drone toward the street and quickly flew to the front of the house. After a few minutes of this I was getting pretty good at flying. As the drone made its way in front of the picture window, I edged it in closer. Then, things started to happen—fast.

CHAPTER 20
Time for the Authorities

I'd been concentrating on the camera's pictures on the laptop screen, but Whiz was keeping his eyes open for everything.

"A truck just turned onto Decker Lane," he whispered. "Land the drone so the driver does not see it."

Land it! Where could I land? I'm in the middle of the front yard, just a few feet from the street. Anywhere I land, it would be in plain sight. Then, I thought, what about high up? I lifted the drone above the roof line and landed near the chimney. Unless they looked to the roof, for some reason, they would never see it.

My hands were sweating, but I did the best I could. Before we could make our next move, the truck pulled up in front of the house—and it was pulling an empty trailer.

"Duck down," Whiz whispered. "And stay quiet."

He didn't have to tell me twice—my parents didn't raise an idiot.

Lucky for us—or maybe it was skill, that's how I'm going to tell it later—the drone's camera was pointing down the roof slope right at the driveway. We could watch the action on the laptop.

As we watched, the driver of the truck backed the trailer up to the DeLorean. He jumped out of the cab and reached in to hit the horn—twice. To our big surprise, Cal came out of the side door of the house. He walked up to the truck and spoke with the driver. Then, he turned to point at the DeLorean. Whiz zoomed the camera all the way in and hit the capture button to save a still shot of Cal's face.

"That is our cue," said Whiz.

"Cue for what?"

"We bring in the authorities."

Before we could move, the two guys walked toward the backyard. Cal was talking away, but I couldn't make out what he was saying, and they both were staring at the car. As they got closer, the words became clearer.

The guy from the truck walked around the car— kicking the tires a few times.

"Why're you selling?" asked the truck driver.

"I'm leaving town and I can't take it with me. I've spent the past two years restoring it, the engine is the only thing left to work on. If I had a couple of weeks, I'd finish it, but I'm leaving tonight."

"Well, Cal, let's go inside and see if we can make a deal."

They both walked to the house and entered by the side door.

"We need to get to a phone," Whiz said, and we both crawled off between the trees.

Whiz tucked the laptop into his Surveillance Kit and threw it over his back, while I stuffed the drone control in mine. We would have to come back for the drone. Without further words, we ran out of the field.

At Jasper Springs Road, we turned toward town and ran full out. We only needed to go about two blocks and there was a gas station with a phone booth near the building. I reached it first and started to dig some change out of my pocket ... then I froze!

There was no phone in the phone booth.

The guy inside the building had pulled his head out from under the hood of a car he was working on and began laughing. Both Whiz and I looked at him. We must have had the saddest, most embarrassed look on our faces, because he stopped laughing, or at least tried to—he still had a smirk on his face.

"The phone company pulled that phone out a couple of years back when they put the cell tower up at the interstate interchange."

"You have cell phone service out here?" I asked.

That sure startled me, because even Jasper Springs, a much bigger place only had service over about half the town.

"Yeah. They put in towers all along the interstate so cars could have smartphone service. We just happen to be lucky."

"But, sir," broke in Whiz, with a pleading sound to his voice. "We need to make a call, and we do not possess a cell phone."

He pointed to a room off the garage. "In there, on the desk."

"Thank you, sir," Whiz replied, and we both rushed into the office.

"Who're we gonna call?" I asked.

Whiz pulled the business card that Colonel Vega had given to him out of his pocket and waved it at me. He dialed the number and waited.

"We found them, Colonel Vega," he said quickly, as someone answered.

I could hear someone on the other end, but I couldn't understand what they were saying.

"This is Whiz Tanner, sir. Joey Dent is standing next to me."

There was a pause as he listened.

"Sorry, sir. I meant we found the DeLorean and at least one of the perpetrators of your robbery."

Another pause.

"Yes, sir. I have photographs showing the same whitewall tire and damaged front fender, and a picture of Cal that may be clear enough to compare with the FBI artist's composite. Joey and I have made a positive ID."

A longer pause.

"Can you hold while we check?"

Whiz put the receiver down on the desk.

"We need to send the photographs to him."

"How're we gonna do that?" I asked.

"There is a computer right here. Perhaps there is Wi-Fi, or maybe the mechanic will allow us to use this computer."

"To send a picture to the Air Force? This is a small town, what if he knows Cal and likes him. Maybe he's even his father or uncle."

"All good points, Agent K. But we must try."

He went into the main garage. I went, too.

"Sir," Whiz started, even before the guy ducked out from the hood of the car. "Would it be possible to use your Wi-Fi to send a photograph to a friend of mine?"

He stared at Whiz for a moment. I though he was going to explode and kick us out of this garage, but he just kept looking.

"My why-five?" The man looked quite puzzled.

"Wi-Fi, sir. It is a way for computers to communicate wirelessly."

"Oh, I don't think I have anything like that. There's a big ol' wire hooking my computer to the telephone ... with something called a router."

"Would you consent to me hooking my computer to your telephone?" Whiz asked.

"You can do that?" he eventually replied.

"Certainly sir. Then, I can send pictures over the Internet to my friend."

"This, I gotta see." He motioned us back to the office and followed us in. "My computer only does e-mail. And, some web stuff for ordering car parts."

Whiz picked up the phone. "Sir, I have a computer right here. As soon as I hook it up, I will send the photographs to you."

He placed the phone down again. With the mechanic looking on very closely, Whiz got the laptop out of his Surveillance Kit and began rummaging through the wires that were attached to the computer.

"There's more wires in the drawer, if you can't find what you're looking for. My grandson set this up for me, and he put all the leftover stuff in that bottom drawer."

Whiz pulled open the drawer, and the corners of his mouth turned up in a little smile.

"Perfect," he said, as he pulled out a five-foot cable.

In no time at all, he had the laptop hooked to the Internet. He started paging through the pictures to get a couple of the best ones to send.

"Hey, is that Chester's DeLorean?" the mechanic asked.

Now, we were in trouble. Is this the wrong car? Was that not Cal we saw through the drone camera? Should we run for our lives or stick it through and try to get the pictures to the Air Force before this guy can stop us.

"We believe this automobile belongs to a guy named Cal," Whiz let out.

"That's him. Chester Calhoun. Most people call him Cal, but his daddy was always Cal to me. He's little Chester."

"Then this must be his DeLorean," replied Whiz, and I could see he was not sure what to do next.

I started to ease myself toward the door.

"If your friend is interested in buying from that thief, he better be careful. That scallywag owes me money for parts, and parts for that car cost a pretty penny. That kid's a thief, and his daddy would be ashamed of him."

"Sir, I believe that is the least of his crimes right now," offered Whiz.

I relaxed a bit and Whiz turned his attention to the computer. He logged onto a webmail site. After a punching in a few commands, he finally hit the enter key. The mechanic just kept staring between us and the computer.

"There," Whiz exclaimed, as he picked the phone up. "Colonel Vega, I just sent the pictures to your Air Force e-mail account."

"You sent that to the US Air Force?" the mechanic asked, with his jaw opened very wide.

"It's a long story," I said, as Whiz talked into the phone.

In a moment, I could hear an excited voice on the other end of the phone.

"Yes, sir. That is precisely what we thought. The same car."

Whiz gave the Colonel the address of the house and the geographic location from the picture. I heard a thank you through the phone, then Whiz hung up.

"Thank you, sir," said Whiz, to the mechanic. Turning to me he said, "Colonel Vega said they would send the military police right over to check it out."

"So, Chester is in trouble with the Air Force?"

"It appears so," said Whiz, without further explanation. "Thank you for the use of your phone, sir."

"Hey, kids," he called out as we headed toward the door. "Tell the Air Force that he owes me money."

"Will do," I called back.

Whiz and I began running again. This time, toward trouble—something we've been doing too much since we started Tanner-Dent.

CHAPTER 21

Distraction Needed

W e ran all the way back to Decker Lane, where I saw another truck in front of the house and pointed this out to Whiz. He nodded and we continued to run. When we arrived at the edge of the last yard, we jumped the ditch and scooted into the field to hide in the nearest clump of bushes. We could only see a little of what was going on.

The guy with the truck and trailer had backed it up to the DeLorean, with the new truck parked at the edge of the road blocking it in.

"Now we wait for the authorities to arrive," announce Whiz.

"Whiz," I said, nearly breathless, "I mean, Agent M, where is the nearest Air Force Base? How long will it take for them to get here?"

"I neglected to research that information, K, but it took almost thirty minutes for them to get to the abandoned radar station after the alarms went off, and we are at least another forty-five minutes from Jasper Springs, if you take a direct route without the stops the bus made. Then, if you make an allowance for speeding with their lights flashing we could drop about fifteen minutes from that, so it would be safe to say they will not make an appearance for about an hour."

"An hour?" I said. "Cal may be gone by then. As soon as he sells his car he may take off."

"Speaking of the car, they must have made a deal already. They are in the process of loading it onto the trailer."

"Ya know, Whiz ... that new truck could be the one we saw in Farmer Zimmer's pasture," I said.

He nodded. "This raises the stakes a bit." He looked around. "We need to get closer."

I didn't want to get closer, but I didn't argue. I stooped and ran quickly through the field, following Whiz, until we were behind the house again. From here, we watched them pushing the car up the ramp of the trailer. Donald was also there, and they had a small hand-cranked winch to help, but it was still going slowly.

"Jackpot," I whispered to Whiz and he nodded.

"Our assumption was correct, K. We must find a way to slow them down," he replied.

"I've got an idea," I said as I dropped my Surveillance Kit. "Let's move."

And before Whiz could question me, I began crawling out toward Jasper Springs Road. Whiz stashed his Kit near mine and caught up with me. We stood up, jumped the ditch, and walked quickly to Decker Lane.

Here, I turned left and walked slowly down the street, pretending I was just a kid walking down the street. Grownups don't pay much attention to kids.

"What might your plan entail, Agent K?" Whiz asked, emphasizing my code name.

"Air," I replied.

Whiz looked up and I smiled. It was my turn to be mysterious. As we came up to the truck blocking the driveway, I stopped and dropped to my knees. Whiz did likewise—then gave me a quizzical look, but didn't say anything. I reached out and removed the little cap on the tire valve stem. I stuck my fingernail into the stem and heard the hiss of escaping air.

Without any words, Whiz made his way to the other tire and did the same thing. I was a bit concerned that the hissing would attract attention, but the other guys were making too much noise of their own as they pushed the DeLorean onto the trailer and complained that the others weren't pushing hard enough. Soon, both tires on the street side of the truck were quite flat, and Whiz and I stood up and continued walking as if nothing happened.

We continued for several more houses before we stopped.

"Did you notice the bed of the pickup truck?" asked Whiz.

"Yeah, something was in it all covered up," I replied.

"It appears to be the same size as the safe. I would guess that they have not yet turned the safe over to whomever is paying them to steal it."

"I wish the Air Force guys would hurry."

"We need to make our way back to the field so we can monitor the situation from a safe vantage point," said Whiz. "Perhaps get the drone up again."

I wasn't anxious to walk back in front of the house again, and I could see that Whiz wasn't either. He was looking farther down the street.

"Just beyond that second house is a yard with no fence. We can get to the field through there."

So that's what we did. We made our way back to the spot behind the house just as they were tightening the last of the straps holding the DeLorean to the trailer.

"That does it," the buyer guy said. "Here's your check."

Cal put out his hand as the other guy handed him the check.

"Thanks, and I hope you get as much enjoyment out of finishing this beauty as I had starting it," Cal said.

The buyer smiled and turned to Donald. "Now move your truck and I'm gone."

"Sure thing," Donald replied. "I'm anxious to be gone, myself."

Donald walked over to his truck as he fished the keys from his pocket. He jumped in and started the engine. Pressing the clutch in, he gave the gas pedal a few jabs. Slipping it in gear, he slowly let out the clutch, and the truck inched forward but didn't move nearly the way he anticipated. He pressed the clutch in and tried again.

"Now what?" yelled Cal.

"Something's wrong," Donald yelled, as he shut the engine down and jumped out.

He walked around to the passenger side and looked down.

"Flat tire!" he yelled. "These tires are only a month old."

"Well, put the spare on and move that thing. I've got a long drive ahead of me and I want to be home before dark," the buyer called out.

"Just hang loose," Donald replied. "We'll get it outta your way. Cal, get the jack out … I'll get the spare."

Cal and the buyer both walked toward the truck.

"What the!" yelled Donald. "The rear tire's flat too!"

"Two tires?" asked Cal. "How can that be?"

Donald screamed at the top of his lungs. "Why did I ever listen to you about that stupid car? We could have been gone yesterday?"

"Well I could have been gone a few minutes ago," the buyer said. "Now put on some good wheels and move your truck."

"Cal, get the spare from your truck. And you," he pointed to the buyer. "Get my spare out while I start jacking it up."

"I don't have a spare." Cal confessed.

"Then get your jack out and remove one of your tires."

All three got busy doing things.

"Now is our chance," said Whiz.

Uh oh.

"Chance for what?" I asked.

"Stay here and get ready to run if things go badly."

With no further explanation, Whiz started crawling toward the DeLorean. He laid flat on his belly as he removed the valve stem cap from one of the trailer tires. I then heard the faint hiss of escaping air. When it stopped, Whiz quickly crawled back to where I was hiding.

"Every additional moment we can stall them will give the Air Force more time to get here."

"But Donald and Cal could still be gone in the truck with the safe before the Air Force arrives."

"Two things are in our favor, Agent K. One, I believe they will hang around long enough to get the trailer running. And two, we now have the license plate number of the truck."

"Three things," I let out. Whiz looked at me. "Cal's last name ... I mean his real name."

"You are picking up this detective thing quite nicely, Agent K," he replied, with a different type of emphasis on 'Agent K.'

Just then, a strange noise came from over Woodhaven. It was the same wop, wop, sound I heard at the county parachute club last year when a National Guard parachute team gave a demonstration jumping out of helicopters. The wop, wop, wop, kept getting louder.

"Whiz! Look!" I pointed at three dots growing bigger as the noise grew louder.

He was already looking at them. Three helicopters, with US Air Force displayed on their sides, zoomed overhead and hovered. One was over the street in front of the house, one over the back yard, and one over the farm field—almost directly over me and Whiz. The air blowing down on us and the noise were both overpowering. As they hovered, ropes came streaming out of each of them, and immediately, guys started sliding down the ropes.

When they hit the ground, they fanned out in all directions, surrounding Donald, Cal, and the DeLorean buyer. Within seconds, the Air Force guys had the three of them lying flat on the ground. One of the guys who came out of the helicopter closest to us came rushing over.

"Are you Whiz and Joey?" he said, as he lifted the eye guard on his helmet.

"Yes," I responded.

"Come with me. Colonel Vega wants to make sure you're safe."

We followed him toward the farthest helicopter which was landing in the field behind us. As it touched down, another guy jumped out and walked toward us. He raised his eye guard and I could see that it was Colonel Vega.

"Joey, Whiz," he called to us. "Are you guys okay?"

"We are fine, sir," replied Whiz.

"A-okay," I responded.

The second helicopter also flew over the farm filed and landed. It became much quieter. The third was still hovering over the street above Donald and Cal. When the Air Force guys had handcuffed them and the third guy, they laid them face down, flat on the ground. Then the third helicopter moved over to the field behind us and landed. Everything got very quiet and Colonel Vega turned to us.

"You guys really did a great job tracking these guys down."

I was too busy looking around at all the guys running around. They were going into and out of the house looking at everything—just like military commandos in the movies. I guess this is where the movies get it. Colonel Vega noticed me looking—my mouth was probably open wider than the mechanic's was back at the garage. Whiz was gawking, too.

"They're an Air Force SOF team," Col. Vega informed us. "Special Operations Force. There's nothing they can't handle."

For several minutes, we just watched. Colonel Vega kept giving orders over his radio, and the SOF team kept searching places. They pulled the tarp off the safe in Donald's truck and several Air Force guys just stood there with their guns drawn. Nobody was going to get near that safe.

Eventually, Colonel Vega turned to us. "My guys radioed that everything is secure, so let's go see what we can make of this."

We followed the Colonel as he made his way through the yard to the front of the house. Donald, Cal, and the DeLorean buyer were all face down on the street with two scary looking Air Force guys standing over each one—ready to pounce if necessary. I'm glad these guys were on our side. Neighbors were standing in doorways and looking out windows.

"Okay, Whiz ... Joey ... take a close look." He gave an order to his team to turn them over one at a time. "Are these the men you saw last Sunday night in Mr. Zimmer's barn and in our building?"

Cal seemed to still be in shock, but Donald had the meanest look on his face. He looked right at me and his eyes burned into mine. The fear I felt the night he was chasing us in the barn came back with a vengeance. For some strange reason, I was more worried now than I was then, but I swallowed hard and took a good look. That was only for show, since I already knew these were the guys. Whiz looked, too.

"Yes, sir," Whiz responded, and I nodded my head in agreement.

"But not that one," I pointed to the car buyer.

"That's all I need to know. Thank you, boys." Colonel Vega started to turn away.

"What?" Donald yelled. "You guys jumped out of the sky to attack us because of these two little kids? What kind of law enforcement is that? We didn't do anything … whatever these kids told you is a lie."

"Well, if that's true, you'll get a nice apology from my General," replied the Colonel. "But I don't think that'll happen. You seem to have something of ours in your truck."

Donald turned his face to me and Whiz as he wriggled against the guys holding him. "I'm gonna get you meddling kids!"

Colonel Vega stepped between Donald and us. His guys still held Donald firmly against the ground, but I sure felt better with the Colonel standing there.

He turned to one of his men and pointed to us. "Sergeant Grant, take these gentlemen inside and get statements from them while we clean up out here."

"Yes, sir," came a high-pitched response.

Sergeant Grant then removed his helmet and— Sergeant Grant was a girl! I looked around more closely and saw that several of the 'guys' were girls. All dressed up for battle makes them all look kinda the same.

"Follow me, boys," Sergeant Grant said, and we followed.

CHAPTER 22
The Cleanup—More Exciting Than the Case?

Whe spent the next half hour or more explaining everything we did since the last time we saw Colonel Vega. Sergeant Grant wrote some notes but also recorded everything we said. About fifteen minutes in, one of the helicopters took off making so much noise we couldn't hear. After a few minutes, we continued. About the time we finished with our story, sirens sounded, as two military police vehicles came rushing up along with a county sheriff.

We went outside to watch as they put Donald and Cal into separate cars. The county sheriff seemed to act like he was in charge, but he didn't interfere with the Air Force SOF team. The DeLorean buyer was sitting in his truck with his head down on the steering wheel. He kept shaking it from side to side. It may have been a grueling ordeal for him, but he was going to have a whopper of a story to tell about this DeLorean for years.

Not long after the cars holding Donald and Cal left, an Air Force truck pulled up. Several guys, with a hand truck, gently pulled the safe out of the bed of Donald's pickup and put it in the back of the government truck. When it was all secure, two members of the SOF team climbed in the back with the safe, and the truck pulled away. Shortly after, the second helicopter lifted off and followed the truck. I watched the chopper fly away until it was a tiny dot. Whiz was watching also—his eyes as big as mine.

Colonel Vega instructed his team to help the DeLorean buyer get his truck out. They produced a compressed air tank from somewhere and refilled all the tires. They moved Donald's truck out of the way, and the new DeLorean owner slowly pulled his truck and trailer out of the driveway. He still looked like he was shaking.

"You kids did a really nice job," Colonel Vega announced. "Brilliant work stalling those two. However, at this point I'm supposed to give you a lecture about how dangerous this was."

Whiz broke in here. "Sir, we at Tanner-Dent are well aware of the danger we accept when we are investigating—"

"Whiz," the Colonel cut Whiz off midsentence—which isn't easy. "The severity of this situation called for extreme measures on all our parts ... we don't send a SOF team, in helos, in country, for a simple burglary. All I'm going to say is, the US Air Force thanks you for your service to national security. And ...

in a few years, if you want recommendations for admission to the Air Force Academy, you'll get them, from the highest levels."

I had to ask. "But, what was in the safe that was so important?"

"Joey, this never happened," he responded.

I thought he misheard me.

"No, I mean this whole safe stealing thing."

"I'm sorry to say, everything about this situation is top-secret and you'll never know any more than that. Take comfort in the knowledge your country thanks you." He paused and looked around, then gave a signal to his team to clean up and head to the last helicopter. He looked back at us. "How did you guys get here?"

"The county bus, sir," Whiz answered, as he glanced at his wrist watch. "Joey, the time is after two p.m. I believe we have missed the return bus."

"No problem," said Colonel Vega. "Have you two ever flown in a helicopter?"

I think my mouth dropped open as far as it ever has. All I could do was shake my head.

Whiz responded in a similar manner but he did manage to utter, "No, sir."

"Load up, boys, we'll fly you back to Jasper Springs."

"Wow!" Whiz and I said, together.

We followed Colonel Vega through the yard and into the field.

"Joey, bring the drone down," Whiz said.

I dug the control box out of my Surveillance Kit and looked toward the roof. It wasn't there! Whiz noticed too. Colonel Vega noticed us looking at the roof.

"A drone? Was that how you got those pictures?"

"Yes, sir," I answered.

"I suppose it was on the roof as we came zooming in?"

"Affirmative," answered Whiz. "Technology allowed us to get high-quality photographs with minimal risk to personnel."

"I'm sorry. Our rotor wash must have blown it off somewhere."

"Wait a minute," Whiz exclaimed, as he reached into his Surveillance Kit to get the laptop.

He opened it and brought up the feed from the drone's camera. We could see a lot of grass and possibly a wall of a house.

"It appears to have landed upright, Joey. See if you can lift it off."

I pushed the lever on the control box, and sure enough, the drone started flying. I brought it about two feet above the ground and turned it slowly.

"I think it's in the neighbor's backyard. Look at the color of the house," I said.

"Bring it home," Whiz said, in his commanding way.

I lifted it straight up, and before long, we could see it over the trees. I spun it in our direction and flew it straight to us. As I lowered it, Whiz grabbed it from the air, and I shut it down.

"No apparent damage," offered Whiz. "Even the camera is in good working order."

We picked up our Surveillance Kits and stashed the laptop and drone controls.

Colonel Vega smiled. "To the chopper, boys."

The last of the SOF team had climbed aboard when we got to the big helicopter.

"This is a US Air Force MH-60 Pave Hawk helicopter," the Colonel explained. "We use these babies to transport Special Forces into and out of tricky situations. Climb aboard."

As we did, they guided us to two center seats where they strapped us in very tightly. These seats weren't like any I've ever sat in. They were metal frames with canvas straps stretched across them. Putting on the seatbelts felt to me like being strapped into a rocket ship.

"Here. Put these in," Sergeant Grant said, as she handed us little foam earplugs. "It's going to get noisy."

As this was all happening, the pilot started the engines and then the rotors started turning above us— slowly at first, then faster and faster. A gentle swishing changed to the wop, wop, wop sound as the wind picked up. Soon, we were lifting straight up, and the crew closed the big side door we came in through.

The vibration was tremendous, and even with the earplugs, the noise was still very loud. I thought the helicopter might fall apart, but nobody else seemed to notice. We lifted off the ground with a sudden pull that left my stomach behind as my whole body seemed to get very heavy. About fifty feet up—well, I really had no idea how high we were—we leveled off and gravity returned to normal. The vibrations remained.

The farm field and houses seemed to fall away as we tipped sideways and turned south. We started climbing again as we flew over Woodhaven. It seemed so small from the air.

Whiz and I were craning our necks to see outside through the windows in the doors. It seemed everyone in town was outside looking up at us. Out to the east, Marsh River Mountain seemed so small, yet skiing down the slopes took a long time. I stared at it out the left window—I wondered if they called them port and starboard on helicopters? I'd have to ask Whiz about that when we got home. Soon, we crossed the interstate and were over open fields. I kept craning my neck to see everything.

Before Marsh River Mountain and the interstate were too far behind, I could see Indian Lake coming into view. As we passed the lake, I could see Jasper Springs straight ahead. Wow, what took an hour by bus was only a few minutes by helicopter—or at least it only seemed like a few minutes.

All too soon, we were circling over Jasper Springs. Whiz and I were moving our heads from side to side trying to see everything we could. Then, we stopped and hovered over the open field of the Public Works Facility where my dad worked. I guess it's the only place in town big enough to land safely. We came down slowly and I noticed two Jasper Springs Police cruisers in the parking lot—along with my dad's car and the Tanner's car. Uh oh!

We landed, and Sergeant Grant unbuckled us. I was kinda hoping we could climb down the ropes like the SOF team did back in Woodhaven. Of course, that didn't happen.

"Thanks, boys," she said, as we jumped out.

I could see a mass of bicycles converging from every street. Every kid in town must be heading here to see why a helicopter landed in Jasper Springs. Whiz and I both paused to look at the growing crowd. Thorny, Chuck, and Tommy, rode up and parked near the police cruisers.

Colonel Vega was already out and rushing over to Chief Reid. Whiz and I hustled over to our parents, staying as far away from Chief Reid as we could. The noise of the rotors prevented easy talking, so our parents didn't yell at us right away. Colonel Vega shook the Chief's hand, then he took turns shaking each of our parent's hands. He leaned in and said something to my parents and the Tanners. He had a big smile on his face even if my parents did not.

Finally, he shook our hands and smiled. "Thanks for the help on this one, guys. If not for you, Donald and Cal would've been out of the country before we even knew about the break-in. I hope we can get enough information out of them to get whoever was behind it."

Without further comments, he headed to the helicopter—waving as he went. All the SOF team was waving as well. We watched as the Pave Hawk lifted off and flew out of sight. When it became a small dot, Whiz walked over to Tommy.

"Hey, could you return this drone to Ray? Tell him it worked beautifully and was well worth the cost of the camera."

I pulled the control box out of my Surveillance Kit and handed it to him as well. We were about to tell the guys everything that happened when …

"Joey," was the next thing I heard. My dad was looking directly at me, with sideways glances at Whiz. He didn't look pleased.

Before he could say anything else, Chief Reid spoke. "You boys are taking this detective play club of yours way too seriously. But this time it happened outside my jurisdiction, so I'll leave it to your parents."

He and the patrolman then went to their cars.

"The Chief is right. Perhaps you boys are taking this detective agency too far," Dad said.

I could see my parents and Whiz's were about to make a decision that we wouldn't like. The Chief had gotten to them. I had to think of something fast.

"But, Dad," I said excitedly. "We just flew in a helicopter with an Air Force Special Operations Team! They had guns and radios and everything!"

Dad looked over at Mr. and Mrs. Tanner and then at Mom.

"Well? What do you think?" he asked. "Clara's Diner for supper ... we give the boys a chance to tell us what happened ... and discuss their applications to the Air Force Academy."

He almost smiled when he said that. Colonel Vega must have mentioned he would write us a recommendation when we were ready for college.

"Oh, boy," I said, as the parents all agreed.

Then Dad added, in his getting-down-to-business voice, "Afterward, we'll discuss the Tanner-Dent Detective Agency. And ... you're grounded for a week."

The other three parents all nodded in agreement.

Grounded for a week? Even that didn't wipe the smile from my face.

We flew in a helicopter!

THE END

For more adventures with Agent M and Agent K,
point your browser to

www.WhizTanner.com

or go to the official web site of the

Tanner-Dent Detective Agency

www.TannerDent.com

If you like what you read, like us on Facebook

www.facebook.com/WhizTanner

or, follow us on Twitter

@WhizTanner

To see more illustrations by cover artist

Alexander T. Lee

point your favorite browser to

www.alextlee.com

Copy or cut the business cards and fill in your own name to become an official Special Investigator of the

Tanner-Dent Detective Agency

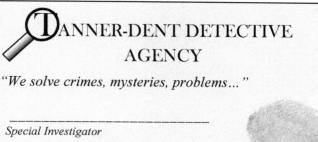

CPSIA information can be obtained
at www.ICGtesting.com
Printed in the USA
LVHW092253170319
610988LV00001B/6/P